A map of the marvelous LAND OF OZ-showing

the celebrated and magical countries

its great protective desert barriers, and many of

which lie beyond the parched sands   Drawn by Professor H. M. Wogglebug, T.E.

Map labels:
- LAND OF EV
- ROSE KINGDOM
- DEEP CANYON
- HOTHOUSE
- BRIDGE
- Isle of Pingaree
- Nonestic Ocean
- Isle of Phreex
- CASTLE
- Track of the Magic Carpet
- Ooga Boo
- Nome King's tunnel
- WHEELERS
- DOMINIONS OF THE NOME KING
- RINKITINK
- Winkie Country
- Woodman's
- Winkie R.
- River
- Truth Pond
- ottenhots
- Mr. Yoop
- Yips
- DEADLY DESERT
- Sand boat crossed here
- WASTE
- PHANFASMS
- WHIMSIES
- RIPPLE LAND
- Kingdom of Dreams
- GROWLEYWOGS
- VEGETABLE KINGDOM
- BOBO-LAND
- VOE
- PYRAMID MT.
- COUNTRY OF THE GARGOYLES
- ODLERS
- Foxville

This book belongs to

_____

who is also registered as

a Citizen of the

Land of Oz

on the page containing

his first initial

REPRINT - BLUE LANTERN PUBLISHING INC. 2010

WHO
Oz

by Jack Snow in collaboration with

Professor H. M. Wogglebug, T.E.,
Dean of the Royal College of Oz

WITH OVER 490 OF THE CELEBRATED OZ ILLUSTRATIONS
BY JOHN R. NEILL, FRANK KRAMER, AND "DIRK"

THE REILLY & LEE CO
Chicago

BY JACK SNOW

PRINTED IN THE UNITED STATES OF AMERICA

What Is Oz?

Literally hundreds of people, from tiny youngsters to mature readers, have asked me "What is Oz—where did L. Frank Baum get the word Oz?"

I have wondered about this myself—certainly never was a more magic word ever invented—and have searched many sources for an answer.

It seems there are a number of answers. First, simply because it has received the widest circulation and acceptance, is the theory that one day, back in 1899, while he had the idea of THE WONDERFUL WIZARD OF OZ on his mind, Baum was using a filing cabinet. The rear tier of papers was marked from "O" to "Z". From this, some would have us believe, Baum got the word "Oz". But for me that explanation is a little too glib and much too prosaic.

Although I did not meet Baum during his life-time, I feel I have spent many years in his company through his books and a careful study of his personal life and times. I don't think Baum's mind worked the filing cabinet way. He was a great lover of Dickens. Could not he have been fascinated by Dickens' pen-name, Boz? Couldn't he have simply dropped the "B", which for him stood for Baum, and used the remaining "oz" for the name of his own personal wonderland?

Best of all, I like to believe that Baum found the word "Oz" in the following fashion: in his foreword to one of his early books, *A New Wonderland,* Baum wrote that for as long as he could remember he had been thrilled and captivated by tales that caused the reader to exclaim with "Ohs" and "Ahs" of wonder.

Oz can be pronounced either "Ohs" or "Ahs".

This is explanation enough for me. Oz came—not out of an office filing cabinet—but right out of wonderland and leads right into another wonderland.

JACK SNOW.

*This book is dedicated
in grateful friendship to*
HORATIO P. BAUM

Contents

	PAGE
PREFACE: What Is Oz?	vii
INFORMAL INTRODUCTIONS to over six hundred and thirty Oz Characters—people, animals and creatures—with hints on the parts they play in the thirty-nine Oz books	3
APPENDICES:	
Story highlights of the thirty-nine Oz books published from 1900 to 1951 (in order of publication):	
The Wizard of Oz and *The Land of Oz*	253
Ozma of Oz, Dorothy and the Wizard in Oz and *The Road to Oz*	254
The Emerald City of Oz, The Patchwork Girl of Oz and *Tik-Tok of Oz*	255
The Scarecrow of Oz and *Rinkitink in Oz*	256
The Lost Princess of Oz, The Tin Woodman of Oz and *The Magic of Oz*	257
Glinda of Oz, The Royal Book of Oz and *Kabumpo in Oz*	258
The Cowardly Lion of Oz and *Grampa in Oz*	259
The Lost King of Oz, The Hungry Tiger of Oz and *The Gnome King of Oz*	260
The Giant Horse of Oz, Jack Pumpkinhead of Oz and *The Yellow Knight of Oz*	261
Pirates in Oz and *The Purple Prince of Oz*	262
Ojo in Oz, Speedy in Oz and *The Wishing Horse of Oz*	263

CONTENTS

APPENDICES:

Story highlights of the thirty-nine Oz books published from 1900 to 1951—*continued*

Captain Salt in Oz, Handy Mandy in Oz and *The Silver Princess in Oz*   264

Ozoplaning with the Wizard of Oz and *The Wonder City of Oz*   265

The Scalawagons of Oz, Lucky Bucky in Oz and *The Magical Mimics in Oz*   266

The Shaggy Man of Oz and *The Hidden Valley of Oz*   267

Biographical sketches of the authors and illustrators of the Thirty-nine Oz books:

L. Frank Baum	269
W. W. Denslow	272
John R. Neill	274
Ruth Plumly Thompson	275
Jack Snow	275
Frank Kramer	276
Rachel R. Cosgrove	277
"Dirk" [Dirk Gringhuis]	277

Who's Who in Oz

A is for ADVENTURE. Any Oz book is your round-trip ticket to adventure. You can travel through strange lands with any of the hundreds of fascinating Oz folks. Read about them in this book—then pick your adventure!

AN "OZ FAN" FRIEND WHOSE NAME BEGINS WITH "A"

One who has tasted high adventure in all four countries of Oz and is now a registered Citizen of the Land of Oz.

A-B-*Sea* Serpent

A curious snake-like creature, whose body consists of alphabet blocks, and whose tongue is a tape measure. With his old friend, the Rattlesnake, the A-B-Sea Serpent once vacationed in Oz. *The Royal Book of Oz,* p. 30 (T)*

✱ The page number following the title of the book (for example, "p. 30," above) tells you where each character first appears in Oz history. (B), (T), (N), (S), and (C) stand for the author of the book whose title they follow: B*aum*, *Thompson,* N*eill,* S*now* and C*osgrove.*

Abrog

For many years Abrog served as royal prophet of Perhaps City in the Maybe Mountains of the Winkie Country of Oz. Then one day he announced that the Princess Pretty Good would be married to a monster within four days unless someone else married her immediately. He suggested himself as the ideal bridegroom. King Peer refused, saying that Abrog was only trying to fulfill his own prophecy. Abrog disappeared and so did Pretty Good. He is next heard from as Gorba, the wizard. (*see* GORBA.) *Grampa in Oz,* p. 98 (T)

Addie

The royal serpent of the Red Jinn of the Land of Ev is an adding adder. Unlike most adders, Addie never adds up to trouble. *The Purple Prince of Oz,* p. 156 (T)

Adora

The Queen of the Kingdom of Doorways in the Munchkin Country of Oz is of small credit to royalty. She should change her name to Ajara, because she jars so many peoples' nerves. Then her subjects could make a bad joke, like "When is Adora not Adora? When she's Ajara, silly!" *The Cowardly Lion of Oz,* p. 80 (T)

Agnes

Known as Tattypoo's amiable dragon, Agnes turned out not to be a dragon at all, but the victim of one of old Mombi's wicked transformations. She now is one of the most amiable and attractive young ladies in the court of Queen Orin of the Ozure Isles in the Munchkin Country. *The Giant Horse of Oz,* p. 106. (T)

Akbad

Because Akbad did what he thought was best—even though his deeds could be considered wrong—some people might call him a realist. Once soothsayer in the court of King Cheeoriobed of the Ozure Isles, he is no longer occupying that exalted position. And he has nothing at all to say—*sooth*ing or otherwise. *The Giant Horse of Oz,* p. 24. (T)

Alberif

On the island of Peakenspire in the Nonestic Ocean, Alberif, Prince of Peaks, and his people, are yodeling islanders. Seafarers, except those who are deaf, usually steer a wide course around Peakenspire. *Captain Salt in Oz,* p. 183. (T)

Alibabble

Grand Vizier to Jinnicky, the Red Jinn of the Land of Ev, the extraordinary Alibabble is not to be confused with Alibaba of *Forty Thieves'* fame. (Besides, there are probably more than forty thieves at Jinnicky's court!) *The Purple Prince of Oz*, p. 153. (T)

Allegro da Capo

Best known as the "musicker," Allegro is a round, fat little man with reeds in his lungs which cause him to make music—of a sort—as he breathes. Since he is obliged to breathe in order to stay alive, he makes music all the time. He lives not far from the Scoodler Country, across the Deadly Desert from Oz. *The Road to Oz*, p. 94. (B)

Alligator

The fearsome guard of the narrow stone bridge spanning the lake of lava that surrounds Mount Phantastico, home of the dreaded Phanfasms, the alligator once was outwitted by General Guph, when he tried to prevent the wily Nome from visiting the First and Foremost of Phantastico. *The Emerald City of Oz*, p. 116. (B)

Ann Gora

This young unicorn is the favorite lady-in-waiting to Queen Roganda of Unicorners in the Munchkin Country. Ann Gora is very pretty, as unicorns go, but we feel we'd rather go away from Ann Gora, her bad temper, and her sharp horn. *Ojo in Oz*, p. 238. (T)

Ann Soforth

The young Queen of Oogaboo, a tiny country in a far corner of Oz, still reflects on her ill-fated venture to conquer the world. Queen Ann Soforth once set forth with a ridiculous army of sixteen officers and one private soldier, confident that no one could resist her might. After many adventures and even more hardships, Queen Ann was content to return with her bedraggled army to quiet little Oogaboo, where she reigns peacefully, happy to be a big frog in a small pool, rather than a small frog in a big pool. *Tik-Tok of Oz*, p. 13. (B)

Atmos Fere

The sky man of Oz is a balloonish sort of person who lives high above the clouds in the stratosphere above Oz. With the help of a pair of iron boots,

Atmos Fere descended to the bottom of the atmosphere. He intended to seize Ozma and take her to his sky kingdom, to prove to the rest of the air people that beings really live at the bottom, as well as the top, of the air. But Ozma had a pin and used it. (These air people think of the bottom of the air, in which we live, as we do about the bottom of the sea.) *The Hungry Tiger of Oz*, p. 182. (T)

Ato

Ato is the eighth king of the Octagon Isles in the Nonestic Ocean, across the Deadly Desert from Oz. His people once revolted and foolishly followed the Nome King in an attempt to conquer Oz. Later, Ato became a cook on Captain Salt's pirate ship. He liked the life so well that, even though he has now won back his kingdom, he spends six months of the year sailing the Nonestic Ocean and cooking for Captain Salt and his crew. *Pirates in Oz*, p. 71. (T)

Audah, Aujah, and Aurah

The three Adepts (at sorcery) are beautiful young women who now rule the people once known as Flatheads, in the wild mountainous region of the Gillikin Country. Many years ago, the three Adepts came to the mountain of the Flatheads and decided to remain there

and try to help those backward people in the use of their canned brains. All went well until Coo-ee-oh, wicked witch-queen of the neighboring Skeezers, transformed the Adepts into three fish and threw them into the lake which surrounds the magic island of the Skeezers. Excitement and magic came thick and fast before the three Adepts regained their human shapes and resumed their rule of the folk once known as Flatheads. *Glinda of Oz*, p. 184. (B)

Aunt Em

Princess Dorothy's beloved aunt now lives in the Royal Palace in the Emerald City. Although there is nothing magical about her, Aunt Em is a great favorite of the Oz people. She is loved for her homespun goodness, her sense of humor, and her never-ending wonder and admiration for all the marvelous people and amazing happenings in the Land of Oz. *The Wizard of Oz*, p. 4. (B)

Aurex

Lady Aurex, queen of the Skeezers, lives in a crystal-domed city on a magic lake-island, in the Gillikin Country. Long ago, Aurex was only one of the serving ladies of the wicked Skeezer queen, Coo-ee-oh. After Lady Aurex aided and befriended Ozma and Dorothy, thus proving she was both wise and good, the Skeezer people lost no time in proclaiming her their queen, in place of the overthrown Coo-ee-oh. *Glinda of Oz*, p. 104. (B)

Axman

The leader of Gloma's axe-bearing soldiers is a man of sharp wit, as well as of keen blade. He lives in Gloma's shadowy domain, in the Winkie Country. *The Wishing Horse of Oz*, p. 163. (T)

Azarine

Known as Azarine the Red, once ruler of Red Top Mountain in the Quadling Country, this lovely, red-haired fairy princess now lives in the Emerald City and is the companion of Ozma, Dorothy, Trot, and Betsy Bobbin. You can imagine how wonderfully her red beauty shines amid the green splendor of the Emerald City! *Ozoplaning with the Wizard of Oz*, p. 204. (T)

B is for BAUM [Lyman Frank]. The first and by far the greatest Royal Historian of Oz, he is its discoverer. Had it not been for L. Frank Baum, we would know nothing at all about Oz

---

AN "OZ FAN" FRIEND WHOSE NAME BEGINS WITH "B"

One of L. Frank Baum's faithful and appreciative readers, who is here registered as a Citizen of the Land of Oz.

Bal

King Bal of the Loons once captured the Tin Woodman, the Scarecrow, and a boy named Woot the Wanderer. Bal was forced to let them go when Woot exploded a number of balloon people with a thorn. King Bal and his Loons live in a forest grove in the Winkie Country. *The Tin Woodman of Oz,* p. 52. (B)

Balloon Bird

This looney bird tried to pick up a little Philadelphia boy and take him to the explosive Kingdom of Balloons. (This has no relation to the balloon town in the Winkie Country.) But Peter let go of the Balloon Bird's leg and made a safe, though wet, landing in the Nonestic Ocean, just off Ruggedo Isle. Then his adventures *really* began! *The Nome King of Oz,* p. 68. (T)

Bamboula

The Imperial Su-jester of Umbrella Island, which may be sailing far over your home at this very moment, Bamboula is a combination jester and advice-giver. *Speedy in Oz,* p. 21. (T)

Bandmaster

Bandmaster lives in Tune Town in the Winkie Country, and is truly "town leader" He keeps things lively in this noisy town, where the police carry batons instead of night sticks, and the trolley cars hum Strauss waltzes. *The Nome King of Oz*, p. 199 (T)

Bangladore

It used to be that giants ate people. But, in the case of Bangladore, who lives in the Winkie Country, it is the other way round. Folks try to eat him, for he is made of a most superior grade of taffy. (Perhaps pulling him made him the giant he is!) *The Royal Book of Oz*, p. 154. (T)

Barber of Rash

The barber once made a hair-breadth escape from the Kingdom of Rash, in the Land of Ev, and found his way to the City of Down Town, below the surface of Ev. He now spends his days giving the money-changers of Down Town close shaves and clippings. *The Hungry Tiger of Oz*, p. 84. (T)

Barrel Bird

Nothing much is known about this bird, except that he appears to have lost his feathers and modestly flies about in a barrel. It would seem that he had been sky-larking and had flown too high! *Lucky Bucky in Oz*, p. 19. (N)

Belfaygor of Bourne

The Lord of the Baron Lands of the Quadling Country once had an enchanted beard which grew enormously. (The thought occurs that the barber of Rash could have grown fabulously rich if *he* had known Belfaygor!) To add to his troubles, Belfaygor was angry with Baron Mogodore—but that's a whole story in itself. *Jack Pumpkinhead of Oz*, p. 85. (T)

Bell Snickle

This curious creature is a mystery—and he knows it. In fact, Bell Snickle is so proud of being a mystery that he won't tolerate any other mysteries around him. Once, he caused a great commotion in Oz, when he "snickled" around the Wizard's Scalawagons, only succeeding in piling one mystery on another. *The Scalawagons of Oz*, p. 41. (N)

Benny

A stone statue of a Public Benefactor—a man known for his good deeds—once stood in a public square in Boston. The statue magically came to life and found its way to Oz, where it soon made friends and was nicknamed Benny. Benny may have a heart of stone, but it is of the soft variety—warm and sympathetic. *The Giant Horse of Oz*, p. 47. (T)

Betsy Bobbin

Betsy is a little girl from Oklahoma, just about the same age as Princess Dorothy. She was shipwrecked and, with her faithful friend Hank the Mule, had many adventures which finally ended happily in the Emerald City. Ozma invited Betsy to make her home in the Royal Palace, so that Dorothy might have a companion her own age. *Tik-Tok of Oz*, p. 39. (B)

Bhookus

This servant of the Duke of Dork lives on a floating castle-island in the Nonestic Ocean. Since Breakfast, the "bananny" goat, came to Dork, Bhookus has very little to do—and he does it nicely! *Pirates in Oz*, p. 188. (T)

Big Lavender Bear

The King of Bear Center in the Winkie Country is a handsome toy bear. Like all his subjects, the Big Lavender Bear is stuffed with a fine grade of hair. He also possesses a mite of magic, by means of which he aided Cayke the Cookie Cook in finding her lost magic dishpan. Too, he helped Dorothy and her searching party in their hunt to find the lost Ozma. *The Lost Princess of Oz*, p. 204. (B)

Bilbil

A long time ago, Prince Bobo of Boboland was transformed into a goat by a wicked magician. As Bilbil the Goat, the prince fled from his native land and became the friend and companion of King Rinkitink, who had no idea the surly goat was enchanted. It took all the skill of the world's most powerful sorceress, Glinda the Good, backed by the magic of the Wizard of Oz, to restore Prince Bobo to his natural form. King Rinkitink and Prince Bobo have become so fond of each other that the former Bilbil now makes his home in Rinkitink's royal castle. *Rinkitink in Oz*, p. 35. (B)

Bill

An iron weathercock perched atop a barn near Chicago, Bill came to life suddenly during an electric storm. He flew blindly in the terrible gale until he landed in the Quadling Country. Here he embarked with Grampa and Prince Tatters on a succession of lively adventures. *Grampa in Oz*, p. 43. (T)

Billina

When Dorothy was traveling with her Uncle Henry to Australia, a storm came up at sea, and she was washed overboard. With her went a chicken coop and one sadly bedraggled yellow hen. The hen, whom Dorothy named Billina, proved to be a wise and faithful companion through a series of startling adventures in the Land of Ev and the Nome Kingdom. Now, Billina is a famous personage and has hatched many little chicks, all of whom she names either Dorothy or Daniel. *Ozma of Oz*, p. 24. (B)

Bini Aru

A Hyup who lives on Mount Munch in the Munchkin Country, Bini was once a clever sorcerer. When Ozma proclaimed that the practice of magic in Oz was forbidden to all except Glinda the Good and the Wizard, Bini stopped practicing his magical arts at once and destroyed many of his wizard's tools. He kept only one charm, a magic word ("Pyrzqxgl") which he had invented. Bini wrote down this magic word and how to pronounce it and hid the paper under the floor of his home. (Although the magic word has long since been discovered, no one in the United States or any part of the great outside world has managed to pronounce it correctly.) *The Magic of Oz*, p. 18. (B)

Binx

Binx is one of the pirates who plotted with the Nome King to conquer Oz. But soon they had the wind taken out of *their* sails. *Pirates in Oz*, p. 61. (T)

Bittsywittle

In Stratovania, high in the stratosphere over Oz, Bittsywittle serves airy dishes and light refreshments to the high-and-mighty royalty of this rarified realm. *Ozoplaning with the Wizard of Oz*, p. 103. (T)

Bitty Bit

The Seer of Some Summit is one of the wisest and most agreeable men in, or out, of Oz. Ozma was so impressed with him that she invited him to make his home in the Emerald City. But Bitty Bit preferred his homey brown castle, perched on a crag overlooking the Nonestic Ocean. Very likely he is still there. *The Wishing Horse of Oz,* p. 226. (T)

Blanks of Blankenberg

These people, who live underground in the Gillikin Country, are called Blanks because they have neither faces nor heads; they appear to be animated collections of clothing walking about. For many years, they held captive Pastoria, the Lost King of Oz, and forced him to act as their tailor. *The Lost King of Oz,* p. 175. (T)

Blazes

Keeper of the volcano that erupts underground in the Land of Ev, the sullen Blazes is too hot a subject to write about at length; we would need asbestos paper to handle him properly. *Grampa in Oz,* p. 144. (T)

Blink

A lovable little Winkie man, Blink is the caretaker of the Scarecrow's corn-ear castle in the Winkie Country, not far from the Tin Woodman's tin palace. *The Royal Book of Oz,* p. 60. (T)

19

Blinkem

The personal attendant to the King of Bunnybury, whose kingdom is a civilized city of rabbits in the Quadling Country, Blinkem, like his whole city, is under the personal protection of Glinda, who is very fond of bunnies. *The Emerald City of Oz,* p. 205. (B)

Blinkie

This old woman was once leader of an evil band of witches who terrorized the good people of Jinxland, in a remote corner of Oz. The two most evil deeds that Blinkie ever performed were to freeze the heart of a lovely princess so that she could no longer love, and to transform Cap'n Bill into a grasshopper with a wooden leg. The Scarecrow, with the aid of the Ork, soon put matters aright. Blinkie was punished by losing all of her magical powers and being sent back to her hovel to live as a harmless old lady. *The Scarecrow of Oz,* p. 153. (B)

Bloff

This fellow is one of the nine fishermen who live on barren Nonagon Island in the Nonestic Ocean. Bloff is still convinced that the visit of the Red Jinn to his cottage was a nightmare, and he still can't explain the disappearance of his poor cat Nina. *The Silver Princess in Oz,* p. 208. (T)

Blotz

General Blotz is a guardsman in the service of Gloma, the dark witch of the Black Forest, in the Winkie Country. It is his duty to escort strangers entering the forest to Gloma's Royal Circle. *The Wishing Horse of Oz,* p. 149. (T)

Blue Bear Rug

Once a live blue bear, this pet of an old woman named Dyna choked to death on a fish bone. Dyna loved the bear so dearly that she had his skin made into a rug. Ultimately, the Blue Bear Rug was brought to life by the magic Powder of Life and proved to be a real nuisance. He followed Dyna all around the house and refused to lie flat, for sweeping. *The Road to Oz,* p. 179. (B)

Blue Rabbit

Blue Rabbit has blue eyes and lives in the blue Munchkin Country. He once led the Scarecrow, the Tin Woodman, Polychrome, and Woot the Wanderer through his burrow under the Wall of Solid Air, so that they could continue their journey to Mount Munch. Blue Rabbit is especially fond of blue carrots. *The Tin Woodman of Oz,* p. 264. (B)

Blug

General Blug, commander of the Nome King's legions of warriors, once gave the old Nome his first idea about conquering Oz. It was Blug's plan to burrow a tunnel under the Deadly Desert, leading to the Emerald City. However, Blug made the mistake of telling Roquat that his armies were not powerful enough to conquer the Emerald City. The wicked Nome King threw his sceptre at Blug and later banished him. Eventually, the Nome King used poor Blug's idea. *The Emerald City of Oz*, p. 17. (B)

Bobo

The Prince of Boboland. See BILBIL, the goat.

Bob Up

This little orphan boy's name once was Bobby Downs. With the clown, Notta-Bit-More, he found his way to Oz from America. Ozma, Dorothy, Button Bright, and all the Oz folks quickly took the homeless little red-headed boy to their hearts, and you can be sure he is living very happily in Oz today, with his faithful clown friend. *The Cowardly Lion of Oz*, p. 37. (T)

Boglodore

Boglodore was a wizard in Ozamaland and was also known as the Old Man of the Jungle. He carried Prince Tandy off to Patripanny Island in the Nonestic Ocean and left him to the mercies of the wild beasts and Leopard Men. When his own treachery betrayed him, Boglodore turned against his co-plotter in a way that helped Prince Tandy out of his difficulties. *Captain Salt in Oz*, p. 260. (T)

Boldoso

At one time, Boldoso was a henchman of Realbad the bandit. Now he is a peaceful Winkie farmer, prouder of his golden corn than he was of his golden coins in former days. *Ojo in Oz*, p. 52 (T)

Bookman

This curious little man lives in the Winkie Country. His body is a book, but it never contains the information anyone wants, unfortunately. (We have tried to make WHO'S WHO IN OZ very different from Bookman!) *The Nome King of Oz*, p. 220. (T)

Book of Royalty

The King of Bookville, in the Winkie Country, is a proud, stupid, and unpleasant monarch. His hard-tooled cover conceals much lore respecting the superiority of royalty over common folk. We would like to tell the King of Bookville that he is out of date—in fact, he is out of print! *The Hidden Valley of Oz*, p. 152. (C)

Boq

Boq is the Munchkin man who so kindly entertained Dorothy, sheltering her in his home on the little girl's first night in Oz, during her first visit to Emerald City. *The Wizard of Oz*, p. 21. (B)

Bragga

Captain of the Guard of Baffleburg, Bragga is like some other minor officials: what he lacks in ability, he makes up in *bragga-docio*. *Jack Pumpkinhead of Oz*, p. 140. (T)

Braided Man

This curious personage is a very old man who lives half way up the spiral staircase, in the Pyramid Mountain of the Valley of Voe, a little-known underground country across the Deadly Desert from Oz. The Braided Man's white hair and beard are so long they fall to his feet. He has very carefully braided both hair and beard, tying them with brightly colored ribbons. He manufactures flutters for American flags and rustles for ladies' silk dresses. *Dorothy and the Wizard in Oz*, p. 113. (B)

Breakfast

Breakfast is a "bananny" goat, the only one of her kind. Her horns are golden-ripe bananas, which keep falling off wherever she goes. So, Breakfast leaves a trail of bananas—which would make her a very welcome visitor to a fruit store. In case you like milk with your breakfast bananas, Breakfast can supply that, too. *Pirates of Oz*, p. 170. (T)

Bristle

In the city of Bunnybury, Quadling Country, Bristle is the Keeper of the Wicket, which is about like being Guardian of the Gate. Bristle, who is one of the exclusively rabbity inhabitants of Bunnybury, greets all visitors and conducts them to His Majesty, the King. *The Emerald City of Oz*, p. 198. (B)

Brown Wren

This saucy little bird once helped the Shaggy Man and his friends escape from a place called Hightown, located somewhere in the sky over the Valley of Romance. The brown wren taught Shaggy and his comrades that there are more ways of going through the air than flying. Ever try swimming in the air? Shaggy did. *The Shaggy Man of Oz*, p. 97. (S)

Bru

Not much is known about Bru, except that he is one of the wisest animals in the great Forest of Gugu in the Gillikin Country, and that he is one of the three Counselors of King Gugu, ruler of that forest. *The Magic of Oz*, p. 82. (B)

Bubbles

These "bubbles" are to be found on the Up-hill-down-hill River in the Nome Kingdom, across the Deadly Desert from Oz. When one pops and vanishes, it speaks a single word. The only disadvantage in conversing with the bubbles is that a lengthy conversation is likely to find you answering yourself. *Lucky Bucky in Oz*, p. 73. (N)

Bud

King Bud is the ruler of Noland, a beautiful fairyland that lies across the desert from Oz. Bud is a frank and merry boy, dearly beloved by all his subjects. Once he was a simple country lad, but a series of amazing adventures made him King of Noland. *The Road to Oz*, p. 236. (B)

Bullfinch

This small bird's bright little eyes don't miss much. It was Bullfinch who gave Button Bright the clue that solved the mystery of lost Ozma's whereabouts. *The Lost Princess of Oz*, p. 156. (B)

Bumpy Man

In the magical Land of Mo, there is a mountain which has an ear, and this ear is actually the Bumpy Man. He lives at the top of the mountain, where it snows *popcorn* and rains *lemonade*, and his bumps always warn him when there is going to be a storm. You may be sure this is one weather warning which is always welcome! *The Scarecrow of Oz*, p. 91. (B)

Bungle

When Dr. Pipt was practicing magic, he tested his Powder of Life on an ornamental glass cat. The cat came to life, but it remained ornamental and not much good for anything. Margolotte, Dr. Pipt's wife, named the cat Bungle. It has pink brains, the workings of which you can see, and a ruby heart which is very hard. Bungle now resides in the Emerald City, but spends a great deal of time tramping about Oz, exploring and discovering odd nooks and crannies of the famous fairyland. For Bungle is just as curious as any flesh-and-blood cat. *The Patchwork Girl of Oz*, p. 43. (B)

Bustabo

This fellow once stole Red Top Mountain, in the Quadling Country. He calls himself King of the Kudgers, a not-too-pleasant people who live on the mountain. Without knowing it, Bustabo achieved a happy result by stealing Red Top Mountain. For it had been ruled by Azarine, a beautiful fairy princess. When she lost her mountain kingdom, she went to the Emerald City to live and soon became a great favorite. *Ozoplaning with the Wizard of Oz*, p. 182. (T)

Button Bright

Button Bright once lived in Philadelphia, where he was always getting lost. Somehow, he wandered right into fairyland and met Dorothy and the Shaggy Man. He was just in time to attend one of Ozma's famous birthday parties. The Wizard sent him home in an enchanted soap bubble, but it wasn't long until Button was lost again and having more adventures. He went to Sky Island with Trot and Cap'n Bill. Since he has come to Oz with the Scarecrow, Trot, and Cap'n Bill, he finds it the best country of all in which to get lost. Someday, perhaps there will be a whole book about Button Bright's doings. *The Road to Oz,* p. 28. (B)

Buzzub

Regos is an island in the Nonestic Ocean ruled by King Gos, and Buzzub is a captain in King Gos' army. Big and burly as he is, Buzzub was once defied, overcome, and sorely frightened by the boyish Prince Inga of Pingaree. The big warrior learned that appearances can be very deceiving, and that you should know your enemy before you laugh at him. *Rinkitink in Oz,* p. 114. (B)

C is for COURAGE. The Cowardly Lion's adventures have taught him that seldom is it possible to face danger without fear. The important thing is that your courage be *stronger* than your fear

---
AN "OZ FAN" FRIEND WHOSE NAME BEGINS WITH "C"

One whose courage will assert itself when called upon to do so, and who is here registered as a Citizen of the Land of Oz.

Candy Man

Made entirely of the finest quality candies, the Candy Man lives in one of the delightful valleys of Merryland, the fourth valley of seven, in all. In this particular valley, the people are all made of candy, as is their land. The earth is delicious fudge, and the fountains all gush lemonade. The Candy Man once accompanied Queen Dolly of Merryland to the Emerald City, where they were distinguished guests of Ozma at one of her wonderful birthday parties. *The Road to Oz*, p. 231. (B)

Cap'n Bill Wheedles

Cap'n Bill is an old sailor who now makes his home in the Emerald City. One of the best-loved personages of Oz, he has been the life-long friend and companion of Trot, a little girl who came to Oz with him. At about the time Trot was born, Cap'n Bill suffered an accident which resulted in the loss of a leg. This ended his career as a sailor. At the suggestion of Cap'n Griffith, also a sea-going man who was away from home much of the time, Cap'n Bill came to stay with Mrs. Griffith to help look after Trot. Thus, Trot found a constant companion in the old man, from whom she learned many curious things about the sea. Loving the little girl as if she were his own child, Cap'n Bill had many strange and amazing fairy adventures with Trot, even before they came to Oz. For their adventures in the fabulous fairyland of Oz, you must read *The Scarecrow of Oz*, p. 13. (B)

Captain Fyter

This tin soldier sadly became a man of tin in much the same fashion as the famous Tin Woodman. Captain Fyter was in love with the same Winkie maiden as Nick Chopper, and his sword was enchanted by the same wicked witch who caused the Tin Woodman's axe to turn on him. And it was the same master tinsmith, Ku Klip, who replaced his damaged parts with tin ones. But, when the Tin Soldier rusted and stood helpless in the forest, it was not Dorothy and the Scarecrow who rescued him, but the Scarecrow and the Tin Woodman. *The Tin Woodman of Oz*, p. 193. (B)

Captain of the Paper Soldiers

Here is one officer made entirely of paper—no brass. He patrols the live paper village made by Miss Cuttenclip from magic live paper given her by Glinda the Good. The Captain of the Paper Soldiers is very brave and afraid of virtually nothing, unless it is a strong wind! *The Emerald City of Oz*, p. 104. (B)

Carter Green

This pleasant person is known as the Vegetable Man of Oz. But he doesn't *sell* vegetables—he *is* a vegetable. Once, he was a Winkie man, and he ate so many vegetables that he turned into quite a variety of them. We hasten to add that this could happen only in the amazing Land of Oz, so don't try to convince your mother that you will turn into a plate of spinach if you have to eat too much of it. However, we do know some carrot-topped boys and girls who may be distant cousins of this Carter Green. *The Hungry Tiger of Oz*, p. 56. (T)

Cat with Two Tails

Tattypoo, good witch of the Gillikin Country, has a cat with two tails. This curious cat has nine lives and twenty-four appetites—one for each hour around the clock. *The Giant Horse of Oz*, p. 116. (T)

Cayke the Cookie Cook

In the far southwestern part of the Winkie Country, there is a high plateau, and on it live the Yips. Cayke is a Yip. When Cayke's magic dishpan was stolen, she and the wise Frogman went out in search of it. This was the first time a Yip had ever ventured off the mountain top. Before Cayke recovered her precious dishpan, she and the Frogman had some pretty exciting adventures. *The Lost Princess of Oz*, p. 39. (B)

C. Bunn, Esquire

As his name suggests, C. Bunn, Esq., *is* a bun. In fact, he's a cinnamon Bun and so important that the Quadling town of Bunbury is named for him. *The Emerald City of Oz*, p. 182. (B)

Chalk

This famous Wishing Horse of Oz is the faithful steed, friend, and companion of Skamperoo, King of Skampavia, near the Land of Ev. Not just because his name is Chalk, but because of his many excellent qualities, the Wishing Horse was bound to make his mark in Oz. He did—and played a large part in liberating Oz and freeing its people. (Chalk up a victory for Chalk!) *The Wishing Horse of Oz,* p. 47. (T)

Chalulu

The official "Wise Man" of the court of Regalia in the Gillikin Country, Chalulu got his reputation for being wise by advising everyone to do nothing. Of course, if you do nothing, you are not likely to get into trouble, nor are you likely to accomplish anything good, either. So the people who followed Chalulu's advice led very safe, but dull, lives. And yet they thought Chalulu a very wise man. We're glad he lives in far-off Regalia. *The Purple Prince of Oz,* p. 131. (T)

Cheer

The King of the Illumi Nation is a hand-dipped monarch, a Candleman, as are all the inhabitants of this shadowy realm that lies just below the surface of the Gillikin Country. These Candlemen build their houses of sticks (*candle*sticks, of course) and King Cheer sits, not on a throne, but on a candelabrum. (Could this be the land from which came the saying, "Don't burn your candle at both ends?") *Kabumpo in Oz,* p. 149. (T)

Cheeriobed

In the Munchkin Country lie the Ozure Isles, and the king of these beautiful islands is Cheeriobed. A long time ago, old Mombi the witch stole Cheeriobed's Queen Orin and placed a monster called Quiberon in Orizon Lake, where the Ozure Isles are located. After years of Quiberon's tyrrany, Cheeriobed and Orin were happily reunited, and Ozma proclaimed them King and Queen of the Munchkin Country. *The Giant Horse of Oz,* p. 20. (T)

Chick the Cherub

The world's first incubator baby is Chick the Cherub, who is head booleywag for His Majesty, King John Dough of Hiland and Loland. (A booleywag is a sort of combination court jester and prime minister.) Before John Dough became a king, he and this merry child enjoyed many wonderful adventures together. *The Road to Oz,* p. 222. (B)

Chief Counselor

In the days when the Nome King was known as Roquat the Red, the Chief Counselor was one of the most important persons at that metal monarch's court. But the Chief Counselor made the mis-

34

take of speaking frankly and honestly to the Nome King and was "thrown away." *The Emerald City of Oz*, p. 12. (B)

Chief Dipper

Centered in the courtyard of the royal castle of the Kingdom of Pumperdink, Munchkin Country, there is a well. Chief Dipper is in charge of this well, into which he dips all those who are guilty of a misdeed, until they are thoroughly wet and very much humiliated. When Chief Dipper isn't busy dipping folk into this well, he dips his pen into a bottle of ink and writes poetry of questionable quality. Thus, we can say that the guilty suffer from his well-dipping, while the innocent suffer from his pen-dipping. *Kabumpo in Oz*, p. 21. (T)

Chief of the Snowmen

The Snowmen of Icetown, in the Winkie Country, are not a bit the jolly snowmen we make in the winter. These Snowmen are disagreeable, unfriendly, and unmelting. The Chief of the Snowmen is the coldest of them all (Please avoid confusion with either Jack Frost or Jack Snow!) *The Hidden Valley of Oz*, p. 201. (C)

Chief of the Whimsies

The Whimsies are big, strong people, but with heads no larger than doorknobs. Since their brains *must* be small, their intelligence is not of the highest order. To hide this, they wear large pasteboard heads with brightly dyed wool for hair and two peep holes in the chin to see through. They foolishly believe that these pasteboard heads actually deceive people! Since Whimsey Land is next to the Kingdom of the Nomes, this was the first place to which General Guph went when he was recruiting allies to help the Nome King conquer Oz. Guph promised the Chief of the Whimsies that if he would lead his warriors against Oz, the Nome King would reward them by magically giving them large heads. The Chief of the Whimsies agreed to do this and marched with the Nomes against Oz. What happened? Well, for one thing, the Scarecrow may have a stuffed head, but there are more brains in it than in all the Whimsy heads put together. *The Emerald City of Oz,* p. 61. (B)

Chief Scarer

Once there was a town in the Quadling Country called Scare City. The ruler of this weird community was the Chief Scarer. His people were called **Harum Scarums**, and they were all pretty frightful—sometimes they scared each other! The Chief Scarer was very proud of the fact that he was born on Hallowe'en. *Jack Pumpkinhead of Oz,* p. 58. (T)

Chief Scrapper

My, what a lot of chiefs there are in Oz! This one is a minor official in the "cross patch" kingdom of Patch, in the Winkie Country. Scrapper met his match when he scrapped with Scraps, the gaudy Patchwork Girl of Oz, who throws a powerful padded punch. *The Gnome King of Oz,* p. 17. (T)

Chillywalla

The Chief of the Boxers in the Land of Ix, across the Deadly Desert, isn't a bad sort of fellow. Chillywalla just can't understand why everyone doesn't want to live in boxes, as do he and his people. The Boxers can't stand the sight of anything that isn't properly boxed, including ears. *The Silver Princess in Oz*, p. 128. (T)

Chimney-villains

These smokies live in Chimneyville, in a place called Soot City. That's a dark spot in the yellow Winkie Country. Since the Chimney-villains are made of smoke, they naturally live in chimneys, and their city is quite sooty. (No doubt they would be just as happy if they lived in the United States, in the great city of Pittsburgh!) *Jack Pumpkinhead of Oz*, p. 37. (T)

China Milk Maid

Deep in the south of the Quadling Country lies quaint China City, where all the people and animals are made of beautiful china. The China Milk Maid is one of the most charming among them. The worst that can be said of the inhabitants of China City is that they are brittle and chip easily. For this reason there is a great wall running all the way 'round the China City to protect its fragile subjects. *The Wizard of Oz*, p. 185. (B)

China Princess

If you've just read about the China Milk Maid, you've probably guessed that China Princess lives in the same town. But she is not very happy there, for she lives in constant fear of being touched by ordinary people. China Princess shudders at the thought she might be broken and have to be mended, thus marring her delicate beauty. Some flesh-and-blood folk are like that, too; they don't know that a few wrinkles lend character and interest to a face. *The Wizard of Oz*, p. 188. (B)

Chin Chilly

Chin Chilly, frigid King of Isa Poso, an island in the Nonestic Ocean, is made of snow and ice, as are all of his subjects. If you ever get shipwrecked, avoid its happening near this island, for it's the coldest place in the world, and its people are all cold-hearted. Any humor they may have possessed at one time is now frozen stiff. *Grampa in Oz*, p. 162. (T)

Chinda

Formerly, Chinda was the Seer of Samandra, in the Winkie Country. Now, she is the Grand Bozzywog of that same country. Please don't spend any time trying to find the meaning of the word Bozzywog, for even Professor Wogglebug couldn't define it for us. *The Yellow Knight of Oz*, p. 64. (T)

Chiss

A giant porcupine who lives in the Munchkin Country, Chiss once had the unfriendly habit of throwing his sharp quills at travelers on the "road of yellow brick." But he went too far when he threw them at the Patchwork Girl (who was "stuck-up" enough without them!) and the Shaggy Man took the quills away from Chiss and sank them in a pond, thus turning the porcupine into a fairly well-behaved citizen. *The Patchwork Girl of Oz,* p. 151. (B)

Chocolate Soldiers

This curious candy army once set out to capture the Emerald City. We suspect that the children and some of the women wanted to surrender to such delicious conquerors. How ever that may be, the chocolate soldiers failed to seize the city, and they were then transformed into tiny toy soldiers. *The Wonder City of Oz,* p. 174. (N)

Choggenmugger

This great beast is even longer than his name. On the Island of Regos in the Nonestic Ocean, Choggenmugger lives on a diet of dragons and alligators—that's how big and tough he is! Once, Nikobob, the sturdy charcoal burner, chopped Choggenmugger to bits, but we learn later that he grew back together again. *Rinkitink in Oz,* p. 144. (B)

Chopfyt

Husband to Nimie Aimee, this surly individual lives on Mount Munch, in the Munchkin Country. Since he was made from the discarded flesh-and-blood parts of both the Tin Woodman and the Tin Soldier, Chopfyt can't be either one, completely. (Maybe he's hard to get along with because he has a split personality!) Let's just sum it all up by saying that Chopfyt is always someone else. The *Tin Woodman of Oz*, p. 273. (B)

Christine

Queen of Crystal City in the Munchkin Country, Christine is barely mentioned in Oz history. Actually, that is just as well, for the only nice thing about her is her name. *Ojo in Oz*, p. 113. (T)

Christmas Tree

A live Christmas tree sounds like fun, but this one provided fun for no one. The last time it was heard from, it was running about the red Quadling Country—where it had no business to be, at all—trying to collect some new ornaments. *Jack Pumpkinhead of Oz*, p. 47. (T)

Christopher

Brrr! is the best we can say for King Christopher and his crystal people of Crystal City, Munchkin. They are all as cold-hearted as the sub-zero temperature of their abode. Let's make our chilly visit a short one. *Ojo in Oz*, p. 113. (T)

Chunum

An aged sheik of the White City of Om, in Ozamaland, Chunum was one of the few people loyal to Prince Tandy, when it looked as if the young prince's enemies were surely going to succeed in their plan to rob him of his throne. *Captain Salt in Oz*, p. 279. (T)

Cinders and Soot

These two are keepers of the dark tower that guards the way to an underground volcano in the Land of Ev. Cinders and Soot escorted Grampa, Urtha, Bill, and Tatters to Blazes, the keeper of the volcano. (Perhaps that's when the saying, "Go to Blazes!" originated!) *Grampa in Oz*, p. 142. (T)

Clocker

The Clock Man of Menankypoo is famous as a wise man. Clocker gives forth his wise words every fifteen minutes—by the clock, of course. Even then Clocker doesn't speak, for his wise words are carried from his clock head by a funny little cuckoo bird, in neatly written notes. Words of wisdom from a cuckoo bird? That's what it says in *Pirates in Oz*, p. 45. (T)

Cloud Fairies

These lovely creatures, with their fleecy, shadowy forms, were glimpsed by Dorothy, the Wizard, and their companions when they were climbing the Spiral Staircase in Pyramid Mountain, to escape from the invisible Valley of Voe. Read about it in *Dorothy and the Wizard in Oz*, p. 111. (B)

Cloud Pushers

Many times, doubtless, you have watched the clouds move across a summer sky. Who moves them? Maybe, if you look more closely the next time, you'll catch a glimpse of the "cloud pushers." *The Wonder City of Oz*, p. 165. (N)

Collapsible Kite

Built for the sake of convenience, this remarkable kite carried Jam all the way to the Land of Oz, where it gained the power of speech. Sometimes Collapsible Kite was very silent, but when a good wind was blowing, what a chatterbox-kite it became! *The Hidden Valley of Oz*, p. 94. (C)

Colonel Crinkle

An officer in the Nome King's army, Colonel Crinkle has a very short, and a very sad, history. Very early in his career, he made the mistake of disagreeing with the Nome King. Just to show he was boss, Roquat had Colonel Crinkle sliced very thin, like dried beef, and fed to the seven-headed dog. Soon after, the dog suffered a bad case of indigestion and *seven* headaches. In a way, Colonel Crinkle had his revenge. *The Emerald City of Oz*, p. 41. (B)

Comfortable Camel

With his companion, the Doubtful Dromedary, the Comfortable Camel was blown to the Munchkin Country by a very severe sandstorm. The Comfortable Camel, who is disturbed by nothing, was soon quite at home with the Cowardly Lion, the Hungry Tiger, Hank the Mule, and all the other famous animals in Oz. Camy attached himself to the Yellow Knight, Sir Hokus, to whom he affectionately gave the name of his former master, Karwan Bashi. *The Royal Book of Oz*, p. 218. (T)

Confido

This Imperial Puppy of the Realm of Samandra, in the Winkie Country, talked too much for his master's good. Of course, his master shouldn't have whispered his secret into Confido's silky ears. He made the mistake of thinking his 'Fido' was a dumb beast. *The Yellow Knight of Oz*, p. 64. (T)

Conjo

After a long career in wizardry, Conjo returned to an island in the Nonestic Ocean with his faithful servant Twiffle. But he soon grew restless and longed for an audience to enjoy his magic and applaud his cleverness. So, he abducted Twink and Tom from their home in Buffalo, New York. And that is when Conjo's troubles really began! *The Shaggy Man of Oz*, p. 50. (S)

Coo-ee-oh

This haughty and evil Krumbic Witch (a *Krumbic* is about seven times worse than an ordinary witch) fought a battle of magic with Su-dic, the equally evil ruler of the Flatheads. As a result, Coo-ee-oh was transformed into a diamond swan. In this form, she lost all her magical powers. Glinda the Good decided this was punishment enough for the former witch, and Coo-ee-oh remains today a vain and beautiful swan on the waters of Skeezer Lake. *Glinda of Oz*, p. 97. (B)

Cook

The good-natured cook was the first Fuddlecumjig to be put together by Dorothy and her friends when the party from the Emerald City visited the village of Fuddlecumjig. The cook advised them about other interesting fuddles to be put together, just like jig-saw puzzles. Later, he cooked the hungry party a splendid meal that tasted nothing like a jig-saw puzzle. *The Emerald City of Oz*, p. 136. (B)

Cooks of Doughmain

Once there was a floating volcano in the Nonestic Ocean. Can you imagine a better place for a bakery? The Wizard of Oz couldn't, so he transported the volcano with its cooks and bakers to Lake Quad, in the Quadling Country. Since that time, there has never been a shortage of baked goods in Oz. *Lucky Bucky in Oz*, p. 21. (N)

Cor

A very wicked lady was this Queen of Coregos, whose husband is King Gos of Regos. She liked to lead her warriors to peaceful islands, to plunder the helpless people. One of her wicked deeds was to make slaves of the ruling family of the Island of Pingaree, with the exception of Prince Inga, who proved to be her undoing. After being thoroughly conquered, we hope that both Queen Cor and King Gos reformed. *Rinkitink in Oz*, p. 154. (B)

Count-It-Up

Where else but in the City of Rith Metic, in the Gillikin Country, would Count-It-Up live? Actually, the Count is nothing more than an oversize pencil, badly in need of sharpening. He's such a stickler for accuracy that he adds up to a *total loss*, as far as fun is concerned. He lives in constant fear that someone in Oz will invent an adding machine and put him out of business. *Kabumpo in Oz*, p. 69 (T)

Cowardly Lion

Although he was a king of the jungle, the famous Cowardly Lion of Oz believed he lacked courage, until the Wizard gave him a super-concentrated potion of pure Courage to drink. Of course, the Cowardly Lion was always brave, but he lacked confidence in himself. That's really what the Wizard gave him. The great Lion is well loved in Oz and has shared many adventures with its people. He makes an imposing figure, crouched beside the throne of the Princess Ozma. *The Wizard of Oz*, p. 47. (B)

Crank Clock

Standing on a stairlanding in the Royal Palace of the Emerald City, the Crank Clock is not too pleasant, as time-pieces go—although you may have known some pretty grumpy old Grandfather Clocks! When you next visit Oz, you won't want to pass more than the time of day with Crank Clock. *Scalawagons in Oz*, p. 18. (N)

Cross Patch

Queen Cross Patch is the sixth ruler of the Kingdom of Patch in the Winkie Country. Her Royal Highness went to pieces some years ago and, according to the custom in Patch, her pieces were carefully placed in a scrap bag. Ten years later, the bag was opened, and out stepped Cross Patch, bad as new. True, she was no longer a queen, but she didn't mind that. You see, the ruler of Patch has to work mighty hard, day and night, to be cross all of the time. And that's very little fun, as you know! *The Nome King of Oz*, p. 15. (T)

Crown Prince of the Lavalanders

When Captain Salt was sailing the Nonestic Ocean, he came too close to Lavaland, a floating and explosive bit of volcanic land. Almost before the captain and his sea-going explorers knew what was happening, the Crown Prince was on board. He had erupted from the island to the deck of the ship. Since he was about to burn the ship, there was but one thing to do. At the suggestion of Roger the Read Bird, Captain Salt loaded him into the ship's cannon and fired him back to Lavaland. *Captain Salt in Oz*, p. 55. (T)

Crunch

Here's the story of a wasted life. A long time ago, a great statue, three times as big as an ordinary man, was carved out of a huge stone. A wizard named Wam passed by and decided it would be good fun to bring the statue to life, which he did. He named the statue Crunch. But the stone man didn't know what to do with this phenomenon called *life*. He just stood still and watched things happen about him. Wam was much disgusted and vowed never to waste another stroke of magic on a statue. Years later, the statue decided to make something out of his life. Unfortunately, he took the wrong direction and proved to be a hard-hearted and unsympathtic fellow. He really got into trouble when he tried to steal the Cowardly Lion and take him to a monarch who collected lions. Glinda the Good and the Wizard stepped in at this point and removed Wam's magic. Crunch is now lifeless, nothing more than a huge stone man standing in the Kingdom of Mudge, in the Munchkin Country. Since Crunch didn't make proper use of his opportunities, he wound up just as he started—a stone. *The Cowardly Lion of Oz*, p. 221. (T)

Crystobel

Realbad the bandit never really was bad, you know. There was always a lot of the knight-errant in him. Consequently, he had to conquer the Blue Dragon and release Crystal City from its long enchantment. But this all started trouble for him. Crystobel, Princess of Crystal City, decided Realbad was just the husband for her. Moreover, she wanted to change him into a crystal man, and this caused him some uneasy moments before he escaped. *Ojo in Oz*, p. 119. (T)

Cue

Back in the old days, poor Lady Cue did her best to give the spellbound actors and actresses on the stage of the Theater of Romance their lines, so that they would know what to say and when to say it. However, she always managed to mix everything up very badly. Today she is perfectly at home, standing behind the players in the bridge games at the Palace of Romance, telling them which cards to play and how to bid. *The Shaggy Man of Oz*, p. 118. (S)

Curious Cottabus

Deep in the purple Gillikin country lives this lavender cat who dearly loves nothing better than to sit on his front porch in a rocking chair, fanning himself and asking

49

questions of anyone who will talk with him. He looks something like an ordinary cat, that is, if ordinary cats grew to the frightening size of eight-year-old children. The Curious Cottabus comes of distinguished ancestry, for he is first cousin to the original cat-who-was-killed-by-curiosity, and to the Cheshire Cat, who live in other books. *Kabumpo in Oz*, p. 56. (T)

Curtain

Queen Curtain reigns with King Ticket as well-loved monarchs of the Valley of Love, just across the Deadly Desert from Oz. At one time, the Valley of Love was known as the Valley of Romance. Once, Queen Curtain depended on the theater for make-believe love, but now she knows what real love is. She is quite happy with her work in the School of Charm and Maidenly Bewitchery, which she conducts for the young maidens of the Valley of Love who are looking for reliable and cheerful husbands. *The Shaggy Man of Oz*, p. 118. (S)

Cuttenclip

Miss Cuttenclip is a talented young girl who has created a charming village out of paper—magic paper supplied by Glinda the Good. The Cuttenclip village is a great attraction to visitors who like to marvel at the pretty paper people. (But if you visit them, beware! You know what a sneeze did!) *The Emerald City of Oz*, p. 117. (B)

D is for DOROTHY, Princess of Oz. Beloved by millions for three generations, Dorothy is the dream daughter whom in real life L. Frank Baum never had

---

AN "OZ FAN" FRIEND WHOSE NAME BEGINS WITH "D"

One who has known moments when trading places with Dorothy or Toto—for a while at least—would have been great fun, and who is here registered as a Citizen of the Land of Oz.

Dad

The City of Down Town, ruled by King Dad, lies under the surface of Ev, across the Deadly Desert from Oz. Dad's throne is a swivel-type business chair perched atop the Fifth National Bank of Down Town. He rules his people with just one law: "Make money." Everyone obeys Dad because, in Down Town, it's the thing to do. Dad has a wife named Fi-Nance who is simply made of money (that's the way he likes her). Dad's Down Town is one of the most wretched places you ever saw, because Dad has never discovered a way to make dollar bills which will buy happiness. *The Hungry Tiger of Oz*, p. 116. (T)

Dan

Dan, the secondhand man, once kept a curio shop in Boston and was instrumental in bringing to life Benny the Public Benefactor. As far as we know, Dan may still be collecting secondhand articles and selling them. *The Giant Horse of Oz*, p. 45. (T)

Davy Jones

Davy is the only wooden whale we know of whose interior is fitted up, most conveniently, like a ship's cabin, with bunks, a galley, a desk, comfortable chairs and so forth. If all man-eating whales provided the interior accommodations that Davy Jones offers, folks wouldn't mind occasionally being eaten by them. In fact, it would prove an inexpensive way in which to travel, as Lucky Bucky once discovered. *Lucky Bucky in Oz*, p. 32. (N)

Daylight

This brilliant girl with the laughing eyes pays homage to Erma, the lovely Queen of Light, in the fairyland ruled over by Tititi-Hoochoo. *Tik-Tok of Oz*, p. 130. (B)

Dear Deer

Dear Deer, wife of Shagomar, the great stag noted for his devotion to Princess Azarine, is the most beautiful doe in existence. She now lives in the Emerald City but seldom makes a public appearance. When Dear Deer does venture out into the streets of the city of Emeralds, all the people and even the animals are entranced with her soft loveliness and gentle grace. *Ozoplaning with the Wizard of Oz*, p. 224. (T)

Delva

There is an underground settlement in the Gillikin Country whose people dig and delve in the ground for silver. They are called Delves, and Delva is their queen. For the most part, both Delva and her subjects are rather dull folks. *The Purple Prince of Oz,* p. 98. (T)

Dick Tater

In the Quadling Country, there is a "live potato patch," over which Dick Tater rules. Most of us like to eat potatoes, but we prefer them fried, boiled, mashed or escalloped, and Dick Tater is none of these. In fact, he hasn't even been peeled. *The Scalawagons of Oz,* p. 204

Dickus

There is a country in the Munchkin Country called Diksey which has had three "Dictators," and Dickus is the third and worst of them. Dictators never get better—always worse—so that when a country has a number of them, the first one looks good by comparison. (Don't confuse this Diksey Land with our own beloved Dixie.) *Ojo in Oz,* p. 163. (T)

Didjaboo

A lot of trouble was once caused in the tiny Oz country of Ozamaland by one Didjaboo, who wanted to get rid of Ozamaland's perfectly good royal family in order to become the ruler himself. Properly, he was one of the nine royal judges of Ozamaland. *Captain Salt in Oz*, p. 257. (T)

Diksey

Diksey lives in the City of the Horners, in the far south of the Quadling Country. A great joker, Diksey once made a joke that was so bad it almost led to war with the Hoppers, neighbors of the Horners. Diksey apologized and explained his joke. When you have to *explain* a joke, you're admitting it was a very poor one, but the Hoppers forgave the Horners, and peace was officially declared. *The Patchwork Girl of Oz*, p. 290. (B)

Dicky Bird

The trees of Diksey Land, in the Munchkin Country, are filled with Dicky Birds, which is no inducement to go there. A particular Dicky Bird distinguished himself by guiding Dorothy and her friend to Diksey Land, but they lived to wish they hadn't followed Dicky Bird's instructions. *Ojo in Oz*, p. 154. (T)

Dipp

Captain Dipp of the Spoon Brigade serves His Majesty King Kleaver of the Kingdom of Utensia in the Quadling Country. The spoon soldiers expected to have a stirring time when they captured Dorothy and Toto. They took their captives to King Kleaver, who was in a black mood and made some cutting remarks. *The Emerald City of Oz*, p. 166. (B)

Doctor Pipt

This crooked magician's fame rests chiefly on his invention of the Powder of Life. It was this powder which brought to life such famous Oz personages as Jack Pumpkinhead, the Sawhorse, the Gump, the Blue Bear Rug, the Patchwork Girl, and the Glass Cat. Ozma deprived him of his magic powers but straightened out his body so that it was no longer crooked. Dr. Pipt was then quite happy to return home to his wife Margolotte. *The Patchwork Girl of Oz*, p. 25. (B)

Dollfins

Dollfins are little, doll-like fish-fairies which live in the Nonestic Ocean and follow every ship that passes through their waters.

They want nothing more than a little girl as playmate. To date, they have had to be satisfied with mer-girls. It is too wet in the Nonestic Ocean for real little girls to play house there. *Lucky Bucky in Oz*, p. 49. (N)

Dolly

A big wax doll is Queen of Merryland. Beautiful Queen Dolly is as large as a good-sized child. Once, two children named Dot and Tot found their way to the Seven Valleys of Merryland and enjoyed a series of delightful adventures in that charming fairyland. Later, we find Queen Dolly as an honored guest at one of Ozma's birthday celebrations. *The Road to Oz*, p. 230. (B)

Dolly

This is the name of another fairy doll, the favorite handmaiden of Princess Ozana, who had this dolly made from a piece of pine wood. They both live just outside the Emerald City, on top of a small mountain on which the famous Story Blossom Garden is located. *The Magical Mimics in Oz*, p. 118. (S)

Dooners

Let's not spend too much time with the Dooners, for they are sad people who live on the shore of the Nonestic Ocean and resent all strangers. They tie up travelers with seaweed and pelt them with sand balls. *The Wishing Horse of Oz,* p. 221. (T)

Dorothy

Dorothy Gale is a little girl who lived with her Aunt Em and her Uncle Henry on a farm in the great prairie lands of Kansas. A cyclone carried Dorothy, her little dog Toto, and the farm house to the Land of Oz. The great wind set the house down in the Munchkin Country, accidentally destroying the Wicked Witch of the East, who had held the Munchkin people in bondage for many years. After countless adventures, Dorothy finally found her way to the Emerald City, where the famous Wizard of Oz unsuccessfully tried to help her return to Kansas in a balloon. The balloon escaped, taking the Wizard with it and leaving Dorothy and Toto in Oz. Glinda, the Good Sorceress of the South, enabled Dorothy to return home by telling her of the magic powers possessed by the silver shoes Dorothy had taken from the feet of the Wicked Witch of the East.

Dorothy made three other fascinating trips to the Land of Oz before she, with Uncle Henry, Aunt Em, and Toto, came to the Emerald City to make a permanent home. In the meantime, Ozma had made Dorothy a Princess of Oz. Dorothy had won all the hearts of the Oz people, and she and her Aunt Em and Uncle Henry were eagerly welcomed by Ozma and all her subjects. The people of Oz feel that Dorothy has brought them good luck, for it was Dorothy who introduced to the Emerald City such famous persons as the Scarecrow, the Tin Woodman, the Shaggy Man, Billina the yellow hen, Tik-Tok the machine man, Button Bright, the Cowardly Lion, and many others.

(It is interesting to note that the first word ever written in the very first Oz book was "Dorothy." The last word of the book is "again." And that is what young readers have said ever since those two words were written: "We want to read about Dorothy again.") *The Wizard of Oz*, p. 1. (B)

Doubtful Dromedary

Doubtful is a desert-going animal, who once lived in the land of Camelia, which was long ago blown off all the maps. So don't try to find it. A great sand storm blew the Doubtful Dromedary and the Comfortable Camel to the Land of Oz. As soon as they arrived in the Munchkin Country, things began to happen, involving Dorothy, the Cowardly Lion, Sir Hokus, and the Scarecrow. For proof, see *The Royal Book of Oz*, p. 218. (T)

Dragonettes

It seems that these dragonettes are not even distant cousins to the dragonettes in *Dorothy and the Wizard in Oz*. Perhaps because these are *Oz* dragonettes, they are kinder and more friendly. They helped Sir Hokus by providing him with something to chase. And you know how dearly knights love to pursue dragons—or dragonettes! *The Wonder City of Oz*, p. 200. (N)

Dragonettes

There are some young dragons who live in a cave under the surface of the earth, just above the Valley of Voe and across the Deadly Desert from Oz. It is the custom of the mother dragon to tie their tails to the wall of the cave so they can't get into mischief while she goes to the surface to look for food for them. Dorothy, the Wizard, and a boy named Zeb once had a lengthy and illuminating conversation with these dragonettes. *Dorothy and the Wizard in Oz*, p. 146. (B)

Dyna

An old lady who lives in the Emerald City, Dyna has many visitors. They don't come to see her, however; they come to see her Blue Bear Rug. Once a live bear from the Munchkin Country, the Blue Bear Rug was brought back to life by the Powder of Life. It is a great embarrassment to Dyna because it refuses to behave like a respectable rug, because it believes it is still a real bear. *The Road to Oz*, p. 179. (B)

E is for EMERALD—in Emerald City, Storyland's most famous capitol. Here, in Ozma's Royal Palace, gather the best-loved immortals of the magic Land of Oz. And here, too, many happy adventures transpire

---

AN "OZ FAN" FRIEND WHOSE NAME BEGINS WITH "E"

One who knows the enchantment of Oz and many of its secrets, and who is here registered as a Citizen of the Land of Oz.

Eejabo

Eejabo, chief footman in the palace of Pumperdink, in the Gillikin Country, once got well-dipped by the Chief Dipper when a certain important birthday cake blew up, exploding the whole kingdom into an uproar. But to find out how Prince Pompadore and the elegant elephant settled the kingdom's explosive problem, you must read *Kabumpo in Oz*, p. 15. (T)

Electra

Electra is a dazzling maiden, one of the most faithful and useful servitors of Erma, Queen of Light. *Tik-Tok of Oz*, p. 130. (B)

Elma

Princess of the Bigwigs, Elma lives in Immense City, in the Nome Country. During the day, while wearing her bigwig, Elma (who is only seven years old) is at least 100 feet high. But at night, when the Princess removes her bigwig, she shrinks to the size of an ordinary child. Elma tried to make a pet of the Hungry Tiger on one occasion, treating the huge animal like a pussycat and dressing him in doll clothes. (Of course, this happened during the daytime.) *The Hungry Tiger of Oz*, p. 166. (T)

Emerald Cutter

When Number Nine came to the Emerald City from his father's Munchkin farm, he had only one friend in all the city. That was the emerald cutter, Number Nine's uncle. The royal emerald cutter did his best to help the country boy in the city, which proves that, in addition to knowing his emeralds, he could recognize a diamond in the rough. *The Wonder City of Oz,* p. 140. (N)

Enorma

A good name, this, for a dragon that once lived on the Island of Isa Poso in the Nonestic Ocean. This fire-breather once made the mistake of plunging into an icy stream. Enorma's fire was put out, and no one ever feared her again. As you may know, once a dragon's fire is extinguished, the horrid creature grows as meek and mild as a puppy. *Grampa in Oz,* p. 154. (T)

Equinots

You've probably seen pictures of centaurs, but I imagine you have never found a live one in the zoo. The Equinots of the Gillikin Country are much like centaurs. They like to keep their stable homes well filled with people to currycomb them and make them comfortable. *The Hidden Valley of Oz,* p. 65. (C)

Erma

The Queen of Light lives in the land of the Great Jinjin, Tititi-Hoochoo, where all the people are fairy kings and queens who minister to the needs of mortals. Erma sees to it with her magic that we of the great outside world have light—sunlight, starlight, moonlight, and even electric light. She once entertained Betsy Bobbin in her overwhelming fairyland. *Tik-Tok of Oz*, p. 126. (B)

Ervic

The Prime Minister of the Skeezers, in the far north of the Gillikin Country, Ervic was once a youth in the service of the wicked Skeezer queen, Coo-ee-oh. After a series of magical adventures, during which Ervic displayed courage, cleverness, and ingenuity in helping to defeat Coo-ee-oh, the new Queen Aurex immediately named Ervic her prime minister. *Glinda of Oz*, p. 136. (B)

Eureka

The pink kitten was Dorothy's companion in some adventures which began in a California earthquake and ended happily in the Emerald City. Dorothy named the kitten Eureka because she had found her, and Uncle Henry told her that *Eureka* means, "I have found it!" And he's right, too. *Dorothy and the Wizard in Oz*, p. 15. (B)

Evered

Evered is the Scarlet Prince of Rash, in the Land of Ev. Little Prince Reddy lost his kingdom, and it took the help of Ozma and the Hungry Tiger to win it back for him. Today, everyone in Rash is much happier. *The Hungry Tiger of Oz,* p. 88. (T)

Evoldo

Evoldo evil did! Yes, he was a bad man, the King of Ev, who sold his family into slavery to the Nome King. Dorothy and Ozma, with the help of Billina, the yellow hen, freed the royal family and returned them to their country. *Ozma of Oz,* p. 59. (B)

Evring

This young Prince of Ev spent a number of years as a purple china kitten, standing on a bric-a-brac shelf in the Nome King's palace of enchantments. By good luck, Dorothy broke the enchantment and freed Evring from his brittle existence. *Ozma of Oz,* p. 201. (B)

F is for FAIRYLAND, old as man's dreams. The magic of
fairyland continually comes true, for man first
imagines, then brings his dreams to life through science and the
machine. Ozma's Magic Picture has already become a
reality in our own living rooms

AN "OZ FAN" FRIEND WHOSE NAME BEGINS WITH "F"

One who has tried the magic paths of fairyland, learned
its secret ways, and is now a registered Citizen of the Land of Oz.

Faleero

A royal fairy princess of the forest of Follensby in the Gillikin Country, Faleero is the homeliest living fairy. She spends all her time gathering faggots, which she stores in her forest hovel. To escape marrying her, Prince Pompadore once fled from his Kingdom of Pumperdink. *Kabumpo in Oz,* p. 34. (T)

Felina

It is well known that black cats are the pets of old witches, so it shouldn't be surprising that snow white Felina is the pet cat of fairy princess Ozana of Oz. *The Magical Mimics in Oz,* p. 117. (S)

Ferryman

This ferryman operates a ferry over the Winkie River. A long time ago, he cut the tail off a fox and harmed other animals cruelly. The kind-hearted Tin Woodman, Emperor of the Winkies, heard of his misdeeds and deprived the ferryman of the power of understanding the speech of animals. And so, today, the ferryman is the only person in Oz to hear only grunts, squeals, owls, barks, and other animal noises, instead of words. *The Lost Princess of Oz,* p. 193. (B)

Fi-Nance

Here is a lady literally made of money—Fi-Nance, Queen of Down Town, in the Land of Ev. But, since there isn't a single coin in all the world even shaped like a heart, no one really loves this poor little rich queen. *The Hungry Tiger of Oz*, p. 116. (T)

Firelight

One of the favorite handmaidens of Erma, Queen of Light, this lovely maiden has smouldering eyes and a radiantly warm beauty. Perhaps you have seen her, dancing in the flames of your fireplace on a cold winter's night? *Tik-Tok of Oz*, p. 130. (B)

First and Foremost

The supreme ruler of the dreaded Phanfasms, who dwell on the top of Mount Phantastico, First and Foremost is one of the most evil of all creatures. He joined the Nome King in an attempt to conquer and plunder the Land of Oz. First and Foremost and his dreadful Erbs wanted no reward; they undertook the venture for the joy of making happy people unhappy and destroying something good. Of course, they didn't succeed. Evil can go just so far, and then it is stopped, of itself. In this case, the evil deeds were halted by an innocent handful of dust. *The Emerald City of Oz*, p. 119. (B)

First Knight of the Realm

In the Valley of Romance, across the Deadly Desert from Oz, the First Knight of the Realm had been in charge of all "First Night" performances in the famous Theater of Romance. The theater is now closed, and the First Knight has a new job. He teaches dramatics in the College of Arts and Sciences in the Valley of Love. *The Shaggy Man of Oz,* p. 116. (S)

Fisherman

This Winkie fisherman once asked Dorothy and Pigasus, "Who is Ozma of Oz?" Can you imagine that? Of course, there was a magic black fish at the end of that fisherman's line. *The Wishing Horse of Oz,* p. 138. (T)

Fizzenpop

The Grand Vizier of Rash is a lovable, effervescent old man who never ceased in his efforts to restore Prince Reddy to his lost throne of Rash. Fizzenpop finally succeeded, and today he is the happiest Rash man alive. *The Hungry Tiger of Oz,* p. 18. (T)

Flame Folk

These fiery creatures are the only inhabitants of the Deadly Desert except lizards and scorpions. Their mirage-kingdom is made of blue flames that grow in the shifting sands where nothing else will grow. *The Shaggy Man of Oz*, p. 198. (S)

Flatheads

There are exactly 100 of these curious beings, and they live on a mountain top in the Gillikin Country. A long time ago, the Flatheads were just ordinary people with flat heads and no brains. Queen Lurline felt sorry for them and gave each one a can of brains. But, once they had brains, the Flatheads couldn't behave. They began to steal one another's brains! *Glinda of Oz*, p. 18. (B)

Flub Blub

This is the name of the King of the Scooters, and the Scooters are a race of people who live on a river in the Gillikin Country. They have great wings in which they catch the wind and sail across the surface of the water, much like the water bugs you have seen in the summer on the surface of pools and streams. (But don't ever call a Scooter a bug! He wouldn't like it!) *The Lost King of Oz*, p. 156 (T)

Fluff

With her brother, King Bud, Princess Fluff rules the Kingdom of Noland, a famed fairyland where strange and wonderful things are constantly occurring. Fluff is so gay and good-hearted that everyone in Noland loves her. Once, she and King Bud visited Oz. *The Road to Oz,* p. 236. (B)

Flutterbudgets

In a remote corner of the Quadling Country, the Flutterbudgets live quite alone in their small village. No visitor ever stays there long, because the Flutterbudgets are an unpleasant folk, who live in constant fear of the terrible things that *might* happen. Very few of these terrible things ever actually come to pass, but the Flutterbudgets talk about them all the time and are always warning strangers of the dangers that surround them. I am afraid that several of these Flutterbudgets have reached the great outside world, where we allow them to walk about freely, alarming those who bother to listen to them. Wisely, in Oz, they are confined to one small village. *The Emerald City of Oz,* p. 238. (B)

Foolish Owl

Foolish lives with a wise donkey in a little house in the Munchkin Country. This is most unusual, for owls are supposed to be wise and donkeys, stupid. But Foolish Owl and Wise Donkey get along very well together, and sometimes the owl's foolish doggerel does show real wisdom. *The Patchwork Girl of Oz.* p. 92. (B)

Forge John

Prince Forge John the First, ruler of Fire Island, which lies just below the surface of Ev, looks much as we imagine a very handsome blacksmith should look. John rules his fiery kingdom, where fireworks are manufactured, with warm devotion. Naturally, he was born on the Fourth of July. *Grampa in Oz*, p. 134. (T)

Fox-Captain

As an officer in the army of King Dox of Foxville, the fox-captain once captured Dorothy and her companions and took them to his king. This led to the working of a magic spell, which had disastrous results for Button Bright. *The Road to Oz*, p. 35. (B)

Friem

When you hear skillets rattling, you'll know Friem is close by, for he's in charge of all the fried foods served in the royal palace of the Kingdom of Pumperdink, in the Gillikin Country. *Kabumpo in Oz*, p. 15. (T)

Frogman

Once upon a time, there was a frog living in a pool in the Land of Oz. A bird picked him up in its claws and carried him to the Yips, in the Winkie Country. There, the bird dropped him into a pool in which grows the magic skosh. The frog ate of the skosh and grew very wise and as large as a man. Then he left the pool and lived with the Yip people. Later, the Frogman left Yip land and became famous, although not too popular, all over Oz. *The Lost Princess of Oz,* p. 40. (B)

Fumbo

Fumbo, King of Ragbad, was so extravagant he reduced Ragbad to a poverty-stricken nation. To make matters worse, he went out into a storm one day and lost his head. His son, Prince Tatters, went forth to seek his fortune and found the head of his royal father. Ozma reunited the king and his head, and Fumbo is now said to be a better king and a wiser man for the travels his head made. *Grampa in Oz,* p. 15. (T)

Funnybones

The settlement of the Funnybones is on the edge of the Deadly Desert, in the Winkie Country. Did you ever bump your funnybone? 'Felt like an electric shock, didn't it? These Funnybones like to tickle travelers with their electric shocks. Like all practical jokers, they have almost no real sense of humor—they just enjoy making others feel uncomfortable. *Lucky Bucky in Oz,* p. 142. (N)

G is for GLINDA, the good sorceress who rules over the Quadling Country. In her great love for her people, Glinda uses her magical powers only to bring the greatest happiness to all. Love is like good sorcery, for through it we bring happiness to others as well as ourselves

---

AN "OZ FAN" FRIEND WHOSE NAME BEGINS WITH "G"

One who knows the excitement of journeying in the Gillikin Country, and is here registered as a Citizen of the Land of Oz.

Gardener

Gardner of the Rose Kingdom, near the Land of Ev, is a funny little man who dresses in rose-colored costumes, with rose ribbons at his knees and elbows, and a bunch of ribbons in his hair. The Rose Kingdom is devoted to the culture of the most perfect roses, and Gardener is a very important person there. He doesn't like people who pick his roses, but the Shaggy Man did—and everyone was happy about that, except Gardy. *Tik-Tok of Oz*, p. 46. (B)

Garee

Queen of the Island of Pingaree, Garee now lives peacefully on her beautiful island in the Nonestic Ocean with her husband, King Kitticut, and her son, Prince Inga. Almost forgotten are those terrible days when the gentle Queen was a prisoner of the wicked Nome King. *Rinkitink in Oz*, p. 21. (B)

Gargoyles

This is the kind of creature we dream about sometimes, after we have eaten too much. These gargoyles are carved from wood and are extremely ugly, and they fly about on wooden wings which unhook from their shoulders. Their wooden country is on top of Pyramid Mountain, rising from the Valley of Voe. Once, Dorothy and the Wizard encountered them, but since the Wizard set fire to their ugly land, there may not be a single wooden Gargoyle left. *Dorothy and the Wizard in Oz*, p. 122. (B)

Gaylette

A beautiful princess and powerful sorceress who once lived in a ruby palace in the Gillikin Country, Gaylette planned to marry Quelala, a handsome youth, considerably younger than the lady and noted for his beauty. The King of the Winged Monkeys, an old gentleman who dearly loved his joke, desired to make the pretty boy ridiculous in the eyes of the people, so he picked Quelala up and dropped him into a lake. Gaylette was so enraged by this that she made the Winged Monkeys into Slaves of the Magic Cap, which was to have been a wedding present for Quelala. *The Wizard of Oz*, p. 137. (B)

Getsom and Gotsom

All queens and kings must have their guards. For this reason, Queen Marcia of Mudland has her two guards—mudguards called Getsom and Gotsom. By the way, you'll have to look far and wide before you'll find another land as unpleasant to live in as Mudland, in Swampland. *The Yellow Knight of Oz*, p. 34. (T)

Giant with the Hammer

This mechanical marvel, built by Smith and Tinker, who also created Tik-Tok, guards a narrow defile in one of the several mountain passes leading to the Nome Kingdom. The giant stands at the edge of the path, beating it with steady blows of his great hammer. This stops many travelers—those who don't have the brains of the Scarecrow or the courage of the Cowardly Lion. *Ozma of Oz*, p. 146. (B)

Ginger

A small servant of Mogodore of Baffleburg, in the Quadling Country, Ginger is a lively lad who performs marvels with his silver dinner bell. When he rings the bell—hey, presto! there is plenty to eat, and the food is always highly spiced, owing, we imagine, to Ginger's name. *Jack Pumpkinhead of Oz*, p. 51. (T)

Glinda

This famous ruler of the Quadling Country is the greatest sorceress of all. Glinda is the firm friend of Princess Ozma; indeed, it was Glinda who solved the mystery of Ozma's birth and freed her from an enchantment that had kept her from the throne. And she has taught the Little Wizard all that she knows about magic. Glinda lives in a handsome castle, surrounded by a bevy of beautiful maidens. She spends her time studying sorcery and devising ways to make the people of Oz even more happy than they are. One of her most prized possessions is the Great Book of Records, in which every event that occurs anywhere in Oz (or elsewhere) is magically and truthfully recorded, just as soon as it happens. Thus, Glinda is wise and good beyond measure, and Oz is fortunate indeed to possess her. *The Wizard of Oz*, p. 202. (B)

Gloma

Gloma, the Black Queen, lives in the Black Forest, in the otherwise-yellow Winkie Country. In spite of the darkness of her gloomy realm, Gloma is a good witch, which she proved by helping Dorothy when Oz had been conquered. *The Wishing Horse of Oz,* p. 160. (T)

Gloria

In the days when a tiny and remote country in Oz called Jinxland was ruled by King Krewl, who had stolen the throne from King Kynd, Princess Gloria's father, the poor princess was most unhappy. And so were all the Jinxlanders. Gloria wanted to marry Pon, the gardener's boy, but her uncle insisted she marry ugly old Googly Goo, who was very rich. What happened? For the present, we'll just tell you that Gloria is now *Queen* Gloria and her royal husband is Pon. And neither of them will ever stop thanking the famous Scarecrow of Oz. *The Scarecrow of Oz,* p. 152. (B)

Glubdo

For a short time, Glubdo ruled over the Red Jinn's realm in the Land of Ev, with the help of his brother, Gludwig. The best thing we can say about Glubdo is that he wasn't *quite* the dumbo Gludwig proved to be. *The Silver Princess in Oz,* p. 202. (T)

Gludwig

Gludwig the Glubrious, brother of Glubdo, was one of the servants of the jolly Jinnicky, the Red Jinn of the Land of Ev. He stirred the Jinn's people to rebellion and forced Jinnicky from his throne. Then, Gludwig showed his real nature, for he proceeded to turn all those who opposed or displeased him to stone. But the little Red Jinn wasn't beaten so easily, and it wasn't long until he had won back his throne. You can be sure that Gludwig received his punishment. *The Silver Princess in Oz*, p. 185. (T)

Godorkas

Lord of a floating castle-island in the Nonestic Ocean, Godorkas, the Duke of Dork, has a great liking for bananas. Now that Breakfast, the banany goat, has come to his luxury island, His Excellency is about the most contented Duke afloat. *Pirates in Oz*, p. 187. (T)

Godown

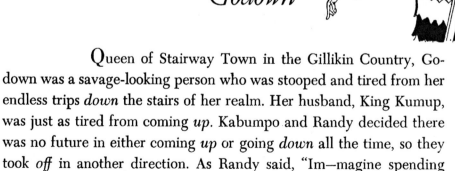

Queen of Stairway Town in the Gillikin Country, Godown was a savage-looking person who was stooped and tired from her endless trips *down* the stairs of her realm. Her husband, King Kumup, was just as tired from coming *up*. Kabumpo and Randy decided there was no future in either coming *up* or going *down* all the time, so they took *off* in another direction. As Randy said, "Im—magine spending your life on the stairs!" *The Purple Prince of Oz*, p. 96. (T)

Good Witch of the North

When the cyclone first blew Dorothy and Toto and their Kansas farm-home to Oz, settling the house on the Wicked Witch of the East and killing her in the process, it was the Good Witch of the North who greeted Dorothy, advising her to travel to the Emerald City to ask the Wizard of Oz to send her and her little dog back home. Although not much has been heard about her since, Dorothy says that some pretty important things have transpired involving the Good Witch of the North, but the story is just too long to crowd into a small space. It would take a whole book, Dorothy tells us. *The Wizard of Oz,* p. 8. (B)

Googly Goo

A rich and powerful nobleman of Jinxland, Googly Goo learned that money will not buy love or happiness. He tried to buy the love of Princess Gloria; in fact, he even paid a wicked witch to freeze the princess's heart so that she couldn't love anyone else. But Gloria preferred Pon, the lowly gardener's boy, and all of Googly Goo's money couldn't change that. *The Scarecrow of Oz,* p. 143. (B)

Gorba

This is the wizard-name of Abrog, if you spell that name backwards. Gorba is the Prophet of Perhaps City in the Maybe Mountains of the Winkie Country. As a Wizard, this wicked man stole Princess Pretty Good of Perhaps City and tried to transform her into a chunk of mud. But the princess was too pretty for that and

 emerged from the charm as Urtha, the flower fairy. After Gorba's misdeeds had been righted, he was punished by being turned into a brown mouse. *Grampa in Oz*, p. 252. (T)

Gos

If he were not inspired to do evil by his wife (who is Cor, co-ruler of Coregos, the twin islands) Gos, ruler of the Isle of Regos in the Nonestic Ocean, would be nothing more than a big and burly monarch, perhaps not too intelligent, but with a hearty joy in his rough island life. He may have grown wiser, however, since he has tasted defeat at the hands of the boy prince, Inga of Pingaree. *Rinkitink in Oz*, p. 122. (B)

Grampa

After he had been retired from active army duty as an old man with one game leg, Grampa sprang into action at the time of Ragbad's need. He went forth with Prince Tatters to engage in a series of amazing exploits that resulted in the freeing of a beautiful princess. When he returned triumphantly with a happy Prince Tatters, he found the love and devotion of an entire kingdom waiting for him in the now prosperous Ragbad. *Grampa in Oz*, p. 17. (T)

Grand Chew Chew

This Prime Minister of the Silver Islands welcomed the Scarecrow when the straw man fell down the Magic Beanpole into their land. The Grand Chew Chew explained to the Scarecrow all about his (the Scarecrow's) former existence as the exalted Chang Wang Woe, Emperor of the Silver Islands. But the Scarecrow found that kinging it can be a royally risky business, and he was overjoyed to be rescued by Dorothy and her companions. *The Royal Book of Oz,* p. 98. (T)

Grand Gallipoot

Directly to the northeast of the Nome Kingdom is the Land of the Growleywogs. The Grand Gallipoot is the ruler of these fearsome creatures, who are very tall, thin people with extremely powerful muscles lying just below their skins. Overbearing and disagreeable, they appear to be thin and weak, but they are really so strong the feeblest of them can toss an elephant *seven miles.* General Guph secured the aid of the Grand Gallipoot and his Growleywogs when he was enlisting allies for the Nome King's ill-fated venture to conquer Oz. *The Emerald City of Oz,* p. 79. (B)

Grand Gheewizard

Imagine! This magician of the Silver Islands wanted to change the Scarecrow into an eighty-five-year-old Silver Islander! The three princes of the Silver Islands were behind the scheme, too, and there was much oriental skullduggery afoot. Dorothy appeared in the nick of time, and the Scarecrow's straw stuffing didn't age even a single day. *The Royal Book of Oz*, p. 206. (T)

Grand Mo-Gull

King of all land and sea birds, the Grand Mo-Gull carried young Prince Philador from the Ozure Islands to the hut of Tattypoo, the Good Witch of the Gillikins. The prince sought her aid in freeing his lovely islands from a magic spell cast by old Mombi. *The Giant Horse of Oz*, p. 40. (T)

Grandmother Gnit

This elderly lady lives in the village of the Fuddlecumjigs, folks built like jig-saw puzzles who are likely to "scatter" themselves at any moment. When she is in one piece, Grandmother Gnit occupies her time knitting mittens for a foolish kangaroo, who constantly loses them. Boxing gloves would actually be more suitable for this fellow, anyway. *The Emerald City of Oz*, p. 138. (B)

Grapegatherer

When Dorothy, the Tin Woodman, Percy, Jam, and the Cowardly Lion were plotting to overthrow Terp the Terrible, a giant, Grapegatherer risked his freedom to help them. All this took place in *The Hidden Valley of Oz*, p. 250. (C)

Great Dragon

This is the father of a family of huge dragons who dwell in a cave just below the surface of the Winkie Country. Woot the Wanderer once accidentally dropped into the dragon cave. If he hadn't been wearing the magic apron of Mrs. Yoop, Woot's wanderings would have ceased on the spot. *The Tin Woodman of Oz*, p. 124. (B)

Greta

Ordinarily, Glinda, the good sorceress of the south, selects her serving maids from the Quadling Country. Once in a while, she is pleased to be served by lovely girls from other Oz countries. Imagine then, the pride and joy of little Greta, a humble milkmaid from the northern country of the Gillikins, when Glinda made her one of her best-loved maids-in-waiting! *Ozoplaning with the Wizard of Oz*, p. 233. (T)

Grumph

With such a name, wouldn't you guess that this fellow is a Nome? Grumph turned up in the Emerald City with his friend Umph, another Nome, and stole Jenny Jump's magic turn-style, taking it up a chimney—a typically "Nomish" thing to do. *The Wonder City of Oz*, p. 191. (N)

Grumpy

When a person is in a bad mood, haven't you heard it said, "He's cross as a bear?" Well, in the Winkie Country there is a cross Kingdom of Patch, where all the people are cross patches. Naturally, there had to be a cross bear living there, and his name is Grumpy. *The Gnome King of Oz*, p. 59. (T)

Guardian of the Magic Muffin Tree

This particular "guardian" has the body of an elephant, the tail of an alligator, and two heads—a wolf's head and an owl's head. Is it any wonder that no one has ever found a name for this creature? But, name or no name, it is said that the guardian is now as harmless as a kitten. *The Hidden Valley of Oz*, p. 48. (C)

Gugu

An immense yellow leopard once ruled the Forest of Gugu, in the central and western part of the Gillikin Country. King Gugu, the leopard, suffered the humiliation of being transformed by Kiki Aru into a fat little Gillikin woman. *The Magic of Oz*, p. 82. (B)

Guide Book

The City of Bookville in the Winkie Country employs Guide Book to conduct strangers through the corridors of this unfriendly city. Since Bookville is peopled by rather uppish and snobbish

"Books," what it really needs is a good, horn-rim-spectacled librarian to put the Books in their places. *The Hidden Valley of Oz,* p. 146. (C)

Gump

Once there was a creature resembling an elk whose head hung on the wall of the Royal Palace in Oz. When the Scarecrow and his companions were constructing a "thing" which would carry them from the Royal Palace of the Emerald City (where they were being held captive by General Jinjur's Army of Revolt) they removed the head from the wall and fastened it to the front of their make-shift flying machine. Then they brought the whole contraption to life with the magic Powder of Life. After the Gump had served his purpose, the head was returned to the wall of the Royal Palace. At rare intervals, this head sees fit to speak, and visitors, not knowing the Gump's amazing history, are quite startled. *The Land of Oz.* p. 201. (B)

Guph

Commander-in-Chief of the Nome King's army and successor to General Blug, General Guph once embarked

on a dangerous mission. It involved enlisting the aid of a horde of wicked creatures to march with the Nome army through a tunnel leading under the Deadly Desert, and then on to the Emerald City. Once there, Guph planned to pillage and despoil the entire Land of Oz. To shorten a long story—Guph is no longer a General—indeed, few Ozians choose to remember him. *The Emerald City of Oz,* p. 32. (B)

Gureeda

Gureeda, Princess of Umbrella Island, very nearly became the servant of a giant—Loxo the Lucky. She is called *Gureeda* because she reads so much and so *gureedily*. However, when she met Speedy and Terrybubble, Gureeda found that her own life was as exciting as any she had ever read about. *Speedy in Oz.* p. 52. (T)

Gwig

As royal sorcerer of the land of the Mangaboos, a vegetable kingdom lying under the surface of the earth near the Land of Ev, Gwig once tested his magic against that of the Wizard of Oz. The Mangaboo tried to stop the Wizard's breathing, but that great Oz personage unsheathed a huge sword and sliced Gwig in two. But he then got planted, so that he could sprout and produce a new Gwig, which seems to us about like sewing seeds of discord. *Dorothy and the Wizard in Oz,* p. 37. (B)

H is for HAPPINESS, ever present in the Land of Oz.
No matter how many millions have
found happiness in this magical place, there's more than
enough for the millions to come

AN "OZ FAN" FRIEND WHOSE NAME BEGINS WITH "H"

One whose happiness requires that frequent hours be spent in Oz, and who is here registered as a Citizen of the Land of Oz.

Hah Hoh

The King of Kimbaloo, in the Gillikin Country, hired Hah Hoh as the Town Laugher. Hah Hoh is one laugher who has both the first laugh and the last—he laughs at his own bad verses, but nobody else does. *The Lost King of Oz,* p. 37. (T)

Half a Lion

A long time ago, a man named Tazzywaller, then High Chamberlain of Mudge, cut a lion in half. The head part of the lion escaped, and Tazzywaller wickedly locked up the rear half in the castle. The unfortunate half a lion (the head) roamed the forests of the Munchkin Country. When Ozma heard of the poor beast's plight, she quickly reunited the two halves and made a whole lion of Half a Lion. Since no one ever dies in the Land of Oz, Half a Lion might have been cut into a thousand pieces, and each bit of him would have had to wander in the Munchkin forests. Of course, if this had happened, it would have made Ozma's task much more difficult. *The Cowardly Lion of Oz,* p. 92. (T)

Hammerheads

These wild and lawless people inhabit a hill in a deserted section of the Quadling Country. They prevent travelers from passing their hill by popping their heads out (like the well known jack-in-a-box) and knocking the traveler away. Except for this strange method of defense and the fact that no one has ever succeeded in visiting their hill to see what they are defending, the Hammerheads are perfectly ordinary folk. *The Wizard of Oz*, p. 196. (B)

Handy Mandy

The goat girl of Mount Mern, Handy Mandy traveled across the Deadly Desert on a rock and landed in the Munchkin Country. A series of astounding adventures involved her in liberating an enslaved king and saving Oz from being conquered. Thereafter, Handy Mandy took her place among the notables at the Court of Ozma. If you wonder about her name, you will quickly learn that she has a great many more hands than you or I, each of them very handy at doing some special task. *Handy Mandy in Oz*, p. 17. (T)

Hank

When Betsy Bobbin was shipwrecked and washed ashore in the Rose Kingdom, her sole companion was a little brown mule named Hank, who was so loyal and faithful a friend that Betsy soon grew to love him dearly. Hank now lives in the royal stable of the Royal Palace of the Emerald City, with such famous animal friends as the Sawhorse, the Cowardly Lion, the Hungry Tiger, and Toto. Like Toto, Hank is from the United States. *Tik-Tok of Oz*, p. 39. (B)

Happy Toko

Once the royal drummer of the Silver Islands, Happy Toko was promoted to the position of Imperial Punster by the Scarecrow. Later, Happy was knighted by the Yellow Knight; a short time thereafter, he became Emperor of the Silver Islands. *The Royal Book of Oz*, p. 109. (T)

Harum Scarum

Harum Scarum of Scare City in the Quadling Country, was a most frightful looking fellow. He continually made ugly faces, groaned and shouted, and he was always wanting to chop off someone's head, or murder someone. But he couldn't scare Peter, a little boy from Philadelphia, because Peter was a baseball fan and had seen the crowds at Shibe Park. *Jack Pumpkinhead of Oz*, p. 61. (T)

Hashem

Hashem is one of the several chefs serving in the royal kitchen of the Palace of Pumperdink, in the Gillikin Country. Without our telling you, you would know, of course, that Hashem is in charge of the meals served on Mondays and days following holidays and feast days. *Kabumpo in Oz*, p. 15 (T)

Heelers

Strange creatures called Heelers once invaded Oz. They stayed only a few pages and then showed their heels to the Oz folk and vanished to their home beyond the Deadly Desert. No one was sorry to see them go. *The Wonder City of Oz,* p. 124. (N)

Herby

The medicine man of Oz was once an ordinary little Winkie man who liked to cure such ills as boredom, fatigue, laughing-at-the-wrong-moment, and other such ailments. Old Mombi did one of the few useful acts of her life by enchanting him, so that he became a real medicine man, with a medicine chest right in his own chest. Today, Herby happily serves as court physician of Ozma's Royal Palace, even though his cures are seldom needed there. *The Giant Horse of Oz,* p. 122. (T)

Hiergargo

One of the greatest magicians who ever lived, Hiergargo built a giant tube right through the center of the earth. When he decided to travel through this tube in order to save time, he went so fast that he came out the opposite end, flew into space, hit a star, and exploded! In brief, he ended with a bang! *Tik-Tok of Oz,* p. 140. (B)

High Boy

The Giant Horse of Oz is an amazing creature, with stilt-like legs that adjust themselves to any length for traveling over a

prairie or a mountain. High Boy cut quite a figure in the Emerald City and proved so courageous and good-natured that he is the most famous horse in Oz, next to Ozma's beloved Sawhorse. *The Giant Horse of Oz*, p. 141. (T)

High Coco-Lorum

The city of Thi, in the Winkie Country, is the home of the Thists, and their ruler is the High Coco-Lorum. These Thists (try not to lisp when you say their name!) are an odd people, with diamond-shaped heads and heart-shaped bodies; their eyes are very large and round; their noses and mouths are very small. The only hair they have grows in tufts at the tops of their heads. And, as you may have guessed, they eat thistles. Until Dorothy and her party visited Thi, no one even knew the city existed, which is not strange, for this strange place is enchanted and jumps about the landscape. In addition, it is surrounded by a nearly impassable field of great, prickly thistles. Beyond this hedge, there is a high stone wall, which is just an optical illusion. From all this, *we* can take a hint—*we* know the Thists want to be left alone. *The Lost Princess of Oz*, p. 129. (B)

High Qui-questioner

The king of Keretaria, a small Munchkin Country, thinks he must have an official questioner to annoy visitors to his realm. The High Qui-questioner does this expertly, aided by a golden staff tipped by a question mark. He once tried to question Handy Mandy, but her answers were so simple and to-the-point that the Hi Qui-questioner concluded she was not playing the game fairly—

93

his game, that is, in which everyone but him is wrong. *Handy Mandy in Oz,* p. 33. (T)

Hi-Lo

Inside a small mountain in the Quadling Country, not far from the Emerald City, there is an elevator that rises to the very top of that mountain. The operator of this elevator is a little wooden man named Hi-Lo. Every day, he carries scores of Ozians up and down. They are all curious to see Princess Ozana's lovely Story Blossom Garden, which grows atop the mountain. *The Magical Mimics in Oz,* p. 86. (S)

Hi-Lo, Mrs.

The wife of Hi-Lo lives on top of the mountain in the village of Pineville, a charming town in which the inhabitants are wooden dolls carved from pine. The scent of the pine and the fresh breezes make Pineville almost as much an attraction as Ozana's fairy Story Blossom Garden. *The Magical Mimics in Oz,* p. 92 (S)

Himself

The elf of the silver hammer appears and does the bidding of anyone who strikes with the enchanted silver hammer. "Himself" is a leprechaun (which means he is an Irish fairy) and a very wise creature. For a time, he and his silver hammer served Handy Mandy and Nox the white ox. He now makes his home in the Emerald City, where he serves Princess Ozma. *Handy Mandy in Oz,* p. 117. (T)

Hip Hopper

Hip Hopper is the champion wrestler of the underground Hopper City, in the mountainous region of the Quadling Country. As with all the Hoppers, Hip has only one leg. We should like to see Hip hopping about in a wrestling match, with all the watching Hoppers hopping up and down, no doubt hopping mad should Hip Hopper happen to lose! *The Patchwork Girl of Oz*, p. 272. (B)

Hippenscop

This young Stratovanian, who serves in the royal court of King Strut, took part in one of the most bewildering bits of Oz history we ever hope to read. Jellia Jamb is all mixed up in it, and Hippenscop turns out to be the little Oz maid's special friend. With Ozoplanes zoooooooming! all about, there is more excitement than we have room to tell about. *Ozoplaning with the Wizard of Oz*, p. 82. (T)

Hip-po-gy-raf

Whatever this creature is, we are sure he is the most hyphenated animal in existence. It takes three hyphens to hold him together. He resembles both a hippopotamus and a giraffe, and he eats straw. Of course, this is all hearsay, for Hip-po-gy-raf lives in the Invisible Land of the Munchkin Country. But one thing we are sure of— the Scarecrow once met him and got the stuffing eaten out of him, but he later found the creature wasn't such a bad sort, after all. *The Tin Woodman of Oz*, p. 240. (B)

Hi-Swinger

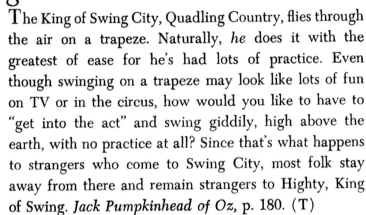

The King of Swing City, Quadling Country, flies through the air on a trapeze. Naturally, *he* does it with the greatest of ease for he's had lots of practice. Even though swinging on a trapeze may look like lots of fun on TV or in the circus, how would you like to have to "get into the act" and swing giddily, high above the earth, with no practice at all? Since that's what happens to strangers who come to Swing City, most folk stay away from there and remain strangers to Highty, King of Swing. *Jack Pumpkinhead of Oz*, p. 180. (T)

His Woodjesty

'Way over in a remote section of the Winkie Country, there lives a "tree man." He is a gnarled old person who rules over the Twigs, a strange, bush-like people. His Woodjesty is the only one who can keep the young Twigs in line and stop them from beating-about-the-bush when they have misbehaved! *Kabumpo in Oz*, p. 222. (T)

Hokus of Pokes

Many, many years ago, right here in the great outside world in England, there lived a young knight. In his first battle, he was defeated. His victorious opponent condemned him to live for centuries in the most stupid of countries. Sir Hokus found himself in the Country of Pokes, in the Land of Oz. There, everything takes a long time to happen for all the inhabitants are slow-pokes. Dorothy and the Cowardly Lion rescued Sir Hokus from Pokes and, since that time, he has been the happiest and most active knight in Oz. He is now known as the Yellow Knight of Oz. *The Royal Book of Oz,* p. 76. (T)

Hoochafoo

This nobleman of the Kingdom of Regalia in the Munchkin Country didn't want to rule his country at all. But, when the rightful ruler was absent, poor Hoochafoo, uncle to the Purple Prince, was supposed to take over the reins of government. To make matters worse, he relied on the court wise man for advice. That resulted in his being known throughout Regalia as Hoochafoo, the Foolish. *The Purple Prince of Oz,* p. 130. (T)

Hook Noses

Hook Noses are a tribe of kilted Highlanders who live in the Gillikin Mountains. Ordinarily, they are peaceful, if a bit dour and unsociable, but when they become offended, they throw their hooks (which they wear on their noses) over the offenders, pinning their arms to their sides. *Handy Mandy in Oz,* p. 107. (T)

Hopfrog Esquire

An enterprising bull frog conducts a bathing beach on a brook near a waterfall in the Quadling Country. Bullfrog is the ideal fellow for his job, and he has certainly selected an ideal spot for his work, for the Southland of the Quadlings is the warmest and sleepiest of all the Oz countries. *The Scalawagons of Oz,* p. 182. (T)

Humpy

In that fabulous Fairyland of Hollywood, in the State of California, where nothing is too unusual to happen, there once was a dummy named Humpy. He was a "stunt man" who performed all those dangerous feats too risky for live actors. Humpy was very happy when he found himself in Oz, appreciated for himself alone, and no longer the dummy he had once been. *The Lost King of Oz,* p. 131. (T)

Hungry Tiger

Friend and comrade of the famous Cowardly Lion of Oz, the Tiger is hungry because he has a longing to eat fat babies. Fortunately, his conscience is many times stronger than his appetite. Dorothy and the other Oz folks who know the Hungry Tiger well will assure you that he would be horrified at the very thought of being angry with a baby, much less devouring one! Still, the Hungry Tiger likes to build up this baby-eating jungle legend about himself, never forgetting, of course, that he *does* have a very powerful conscience.

Most Oz-readers believe that the Hungry Tiger first appeared in *Ozma of Oz*, but *we* think he *may* have been introduced in *The Wizard of Oz*. In that book, (see page 193) the Cowardly Lion answered a tiger's pleas for help and destroyed a beast which had been devouring the forest animals. The Lion promised this tiger that, once Dorothy was safely on her way home, he would return to the forest and become King of the Beasts. We can conclude that the Lion did this, for he does not appear in the second Oz book, *The Land of Oz*. But, in the third Oz book, *Ozma of Oz*, the Cowardly Lion reappears with a friend, the Hungry Tiger, both of them arriving in the Emerald City (where they still live) from the jungle. Do you agree with our "supposes"? *The Wizard of Oz*, p. 193. (B)

Hurrywurree

The Chief Counselor of the Quix, of Quick City in the Winkie Country, is Hurrywurree the Worst. You'll want to hurry through Quick City as quickly as you can, for the Quix are, without doubt, the most unpleasant and disagreeable people in all Oz. *The Yellow Knight of Oz*, p. 163. (T)

Hyacinth

This lady was Queen of Uptown and wife of Joe King when we first met her in *this* Oz book. But Joe was due for a promotion and, in later Oz books, became King of the Gillikins. No matter what her station, Queen Hyacinth is always gracious and gentle. *The Giant Horse of Oz*, p. 151. (T)

I is for IMPASSABLE, the Deadly Desert barrier around Oz.
L. Frank Baum used to make motor trips to
California. Was it as he crossed the great sandy wastes of
desert that he had his first sight of an incredible
mirage—the enchanted scene we now
know as the famous story book land of Oz?

AN "OZ FAN" FRIEND WHOSE NAME BEGINS WITH "I"

One who knows the awe in which the Impassable Barrier is held and who is now a registered Citizen of the Land of Oz.

Ianu

Ianu is a little girl who lives with her mother, father and brother in the Valley of Voe, where all the people are invisible because they eat of the Dama fruit. The Voe people have chosen this diet, not only because it is so delicious, but because it makes them invisible and thus safe from attacks by the ferocious invisible bears of Voe. (Because Adam ate of the forbidden fruit, perhaps the people of Voe have named their fruit after him. If you rearrange the letters in *Dama,* you can easily spell *Adam.*) *Dorothy and the Wizard in Oz,* p. 95. (B)

Imperial Persuader

Although he hoped to be able to tell people what to do and make them want to do it, the Imperial Persuader was only mildly successful, even in his native country of Keretaria. *Handy Mandy in Oz,* p. 32. (T)

Imperial Squawmos

Under the spell of this wicked "cookywitch," an entire village was pickled, preserved and jarred. The Cowardly Lion and company narrowly escaped being canned as mincemeat. *The Cowardly Lion of Oz,* p. 215. (T)

Inga

The boy prince of Pingaree was the hero of some of the strangest and most exciting adventures in Oz history. With the aid of three magic pearls, a fat and jolly king named Rinkitink, and a goat called Bilbil, Prince Inga conquered two islands ruled by a fierce warrior king and queen and almost overcame the power of the infamous Nome King. He did all this in his efforts to free his beloved father and mother, the rulers, and their enslaved people. Inga's bravery and courage brought aid quickly from Ozma. *Rinkitink in Oz*, p. 21. (B)

Ippty

Here's one royal scribe with whom we wouldn't change places. Ippty was once royal historian and scribe of the Kingdom of Rash, in the Land of Ev. One unhappy day, he stole the Hungry Tiger of Oz, whom he hoped to persuade to devour the innocent prisoners of the wicked Pasha of Rash. And that's one idea Ippty shouldn't have popped up with, for it bounced him right out of Rash onto a lonely island in the Nonestic Ocean. *The Hungry Tiger of Oz*, p. 16. (T)

Isomere

Isomere is a fairytale princess who is, even now, living the "happy ever after" part of her life. There was a time, though, when Isomere's husband was known as Realbad the Bandit, and she didn't even know where her son was. We know, of course, that her son's name is Ojo, and that he is now the Prince of Seebania. *Ojo in Oz*, p. 287 (T)

Iva

Matiah the wizard captured Iva, a young kitchen boy, and held him captive in the Nome King's tunnel, under the Emerald City. Iva escaped and played a large part in liberating Ozma and putting Matiah out of business as a wizard. *The Wishing Horse of Oz*, p. 253. (T)

I-wish-I-was

Just above the Munchkin Country is the Country of Un. Its former king had the unlikely name of I-wish-I-was. The Uns have the heads of birds, with brightly colored feathers, and the bodies of human beings; hence, they are called Featherheads. For the most part, the Uns are a most unpleasant people. The only good Un, who is now their king, is Unselfish. *The Cowardly Lion of Oz*, p. 137. (T)

J is for JACK—Jack Pumpkinhead, the first friend and companion of Tip. Made by a mischievous boy and brought to life by an old witch, good-natured Jack masquerades as a man with a pumpkin head and is a Hallowe'en prank all in himself

---

AN "OZ FAN" FRIEND WHOSE NAME BEGINS WITH "J"

One who can enjoy the Jack Pumpkinheads of *any* world, for their warm and simple selves, and who is now a registered Citizen of the Land of Oz.

Jack Pott

A kettle-like king of a tiny checkerboard land in the Winkie Country, Jack Pott is perhaps the most hospitable ruler in Oz. If his visitors will only stay and play a few games of checkers with him, he will pour them the drink of their choice—tea, milk, coffee, or chocolate, iced or hot depending on the season. Of course, if one stayed too long, he might drink so much he'd get to feeling like an over-filled pot—and maybe he'd be a little checker "bored"! *Lucky Bucky in Oz*, p. 170. (N)

Jack Pumpkinhead

Fashioned from sticks of wood with a pumpkin for a head, Jack was made by Tip to frighten old Mombi, the witch. However, Mombi was not frightened; instead, she used Jack to test her magic Powder of Life, which she had just acquired from a crooked magician. Much to her surprise—for Mombi had suspected that the crooked magician had cheated her—Jack came very much to life. From then on, the Pumpkinhead's life was crowded with adventures. The first friend he found was Ozma, and he still looks upon the Little Wizard as a sort of "parent". Early in his career, Jack's chief fear was that he would live only until his head spoiled or fell off the spike on which it rested and got smashed. Happily, he soon found that he could carve a new head from a fresh pumpkin whenever he needed one. Jack Pumpkinhead may not be the wisest man in Oz, but his good qualities are so many and so endearing that everyone loves him. There are worse things to have in one's head than pumpkin seeds! *The Land of Oz.* p. 20. (B)

Jaguar

A jaguar once happened upon the Scarecrow, the Tin Woodman, Polychrome, and Woot the Wanderer as they were adventuring through the Winkie Country. The poor beast hadn't eaten for days, and he felt he would be compelled to eat either Woot or Polychrome, much as the travelers interested him. He preferred Woot, for he feared that Polychrome, because of being the Rainbow's daughter, might be rather soggy and misty. Polychrome helped him out of this dilemma by preparing a magic breakfast of scrambled eggs and toast. Since the magical omelette consisted of five dozen eggs, with two dozen loaves of bread on the side, the jaguar was quite satisfied and very happy to be friendly. *The Tin Woodman of Oz*, p. 113. (B)

Jak

The Horners, whose chief is named Jak, live in a cave city in the mountainous southern part of the Quadling Country. Jak thought it a great joke on the Hoppers (who have only one leg per person) to say that their *understanding* was less than that of the Horners. But the pun didn't pan out, and Jak couldn't understand why! (For goodness sake, don't confuse this Jak Horner from a corner of Oz with the Jack Horner in his corner of Mother Gooseland! They aren't even cousins-twenty-times-removed.) *The Patchwork Girl of Oz*, p. 284. (B)

Jam

From his home in Ohio, small Jam traveled to the Land of Oz in a crate attached to a Collapsible Kite. Among his Oz adventures were the conquering of Terp, the Terrible Giant, and the freeing of the people of the Hidden Valley, in the Gillikin Country, from Terp's terrible power. When his adventures were over, Jam wanted to go back home to Ohio. The Wizard, who had once traveled in that state with a circus, knew exactly where to return Jam, and back to Ohio sailed boy and Kite. *The Hidden Valley of Oz*, p. 17. (C)

Jazzma

Tune Town, in the Winkie Country, is ruled by Queen Jazzma, who has very short hair and a rather loud voice. Some of the older residents of Tune Town complain that Jazzma is much too modern for their taste. (And it is whispered that Jazzma, herself, is now worried about a saucy young upstart named Bee-Bopma who has just come to Tune Town and is even noisier and less melodious than Jazzma.) *The Nome King of Oz*, p. 202. (T)

Jellia Jamb

Ever since Ozma became ruler of the Land of Oz, her personal maid and companion has been Jellia Jamb, and a great friendship has grown up between the two girls. Pretty, lively, and always faithful, Jellia is one of the best-known and best-loved personages in the royal palace of the Emerald City. You will recall that Jellia was a member of the royal staff even before Ozma was princess. She acted as interpreter for the Scarecrow and Jack Pumpkinhead when Jack felt he couldn't understand Scarecrow language. *The Land of Oz,* p. 77. (B)

Jenny Jump

When Jenny was angry, she jumped. Her anger on one occasion was so great that she jumped all the way from her home in New Jersey to the Land of Oz, bringing with her a bad temper and a bit of magic given her by a leprechaun from Weehawken. No sooner had she arrived than she decided to rule Oz. She organized the first Oz election and was ready to run against Ozma. Finally, for the good of Jenny *and* Oz, it was decided that her propensity for ill temper, envy, and ambition had to be changed, and this the Wizard brought about. Jenny still jumps, however; the last time she was heard of, she had jumped down to the age of eleven. *The Wonder City of Oz,* p. 17. (N)

J. Glegg

As wizards go, Glegg was a pretty bad sort, for he mixed his magic so that it mixed up everything. He made plenty of trouble for the ruling families of Pumperdink and Sun Top Mountain, in the Gillikin Country, and he mixed up everything at Ozma's Royal Palace, too. But J. Glegg found that Mixed Magic is nothing to mix into, for he ended his dark career in the darkest fashion imaginable—as a heap of black soot. *Kabumpo in Oz,* p. 286. (T)

Jim

After many years of pulling a heavy cab over city streets, Jim the cab horse was retired to the Hugson Ranch in California, where he pulled only the light ranch buggy. On this same ranch worked Zeb, a young boy whose uncle was Bill Hugson (also Dorothy's uncle). When Zeb hitched Jim to the buggy and went to the railroad stop to meet Dorothy and take her to the Hugson ranch, he didn't anticipate the earthquake that threw Dorothy, Eureka, Jim, and Zeb into a great crack in the earth's surface—the "opener" of such adventures as Zeb and Jim had never dreamed could happen. Finally, they arrived safely in the Emerald City, where Jim made the mistake of running a race with the tireless Sawhorse. Poor Jim was so humiliated at being beaten by a wooden horse that he wanted to get back to ranch life, where there would be no wooden steeds, and Zeb, too, decided he was better fitted to be a rancher in California than an adventurer in Oz. So Dorothy used the Magic Belt to send them back to the Hugson ranch. *Dorothy and the Wizard in Oz*, p. 16. (B)

Jinjur

Jinjur, a vivacious young girl, once raised an army composed of pretty maids from all four Oz countries. Armed with hatpins, the Army of Revolt moved on the Emerald City and succeeded in driving the Scarecrow from the throne, in the days before Ozma came to rule. It was Jinjur's idea that Oz had been too long ruled by men, who were now to stay home and do housework. But Jinjur made the mistake of allying herself to old Mombi. Glinda the Good then stepped in and ended General Jinjur's career as a lady soldier. Jinjur is now happily married and on the best of terms with the Scarecrow, Ozma, and other Oz folks whom she once opposed. *The Land of Oz*, p. 83. (B)

Jinnicky

In his kingdom in the Land of Ev, across the Deadly Desert from Oz, the Red Jinn lives in a jar stuffed full of magic. Jinnicky is a thoroughly likeable fellow and uses his magic to help everyone whose cause is just. Once, he traveled to the Land of Oz to help the Purple Prince free the royal family of Pumperdink. Our Jinnicky prefers to live in a jar, he says. The truth of the matter is that the Red Jinn is so plump no bottle would fit him. But a jar—that's mighty comfortable for a roly poly Jinn. *The Purple Prince of Oz*, p. 140. (T)

Jo Apple, Etc.

This may not be very *Who's Who-ish*, but we're going to put right here all the members of Queen Anne's Oogabooian Army who are named Jo. When Queen Anne set out to conque Oz, she enlisted all the men in her tiny kingdom except one. They were commissioned as follows: as Generals: Jo Apple, Joe Bun, Joe Cone, and Jo Clock; as Colonels: Jo Plum, Jo Egg, Jo Banjo, and Jo Cheese; as

Mayors: Jo Nail, Jo Cake, Jo Ham, and Jo Stockings; as Captains: Jo Sandwich, Jo Padlock, Jo Sundae, and Jo Buttons. Jo Files became, for a short time, the only private in the army, and every army must have its "private files," you know. The one Jo who refused to go to war was Jo Candy, for he felt he must stay home to harvest his crop of Jackson balls, lemon drops, bon-bons, and chocolate creams, so that the children of Oogaboo would not be disappointed. As you may have guessed, each of these Jos grew in his own orchard the thing for which he was named. *Tik-Tok of Oz*, pp. 17, 18, 19, and 20. (B)

Joe King

Once a mountaineer in the Gillikin Country and King of the Uplanders of Uptown, a sky city of Oz, Joe King lent his famous steed, the Giant Horse, to young Prince Philador, so that the prince might liberate his country from bondage. Joe is now King of the Gillikins, and what a merry monarch he is! *The Giant Horse of Oz*, p. 137. (T)

Joker

Mr. Joker is a funny little clown who lives in the China Village in the Quadling Country. Since he is made of china and is very brittle, it is no wonder that Mr. Joker is a little cracked. But the cracks in his head seem to make him all the funnier as a clown. *The Wizard of Oz*, p. 187. (B)

John Dough

John Dough the First, King of the Two Kingdoms of Hiland and Loland, is made entirely of delicious gingerbread, and he was brought to life by an Arabian "elixir of life." Before becoming king of the twin countries that lie just over the Desert from Oz, John Dough enjoyed many wonderful adventures in the company of Para Bruin the rubber bear, and Chick the Cherub, in the country of Mifkets and with the fairy Beaver King on the Isle of Phreex. John is so good-natured that he once allowed part of himself to be eaten so that a sweet little princess might be restored to health by the Magic Elixir he contains. *The Road to Oz,* p. 220. (B)

Johnny Cake

Johnny Cake may have been a runaway when you first heard about him, but now he is a cheerful old gentleman who lives in the town of Bunbury, Quadling Country. He has traveled a lot, being well known outside Oz, and he loves to tell long-winded tales of his adventures. The fresher Bunbury folk are of the private opinion that Johnny is getting a trifle stale. *The Emerald City of Oz,* p. 188. (B)

Johnny Dooit

This fairy friend of the Shaggy Man is never without his chest of tools. Working cheerfully and swiftly, Johnny Dooit can build almost anything out of nothing, in almost no time at all. Once, Johnny built a sandboat that carried Shaggy and his friends safely across the Deadly Desert to Oz. Later, Ozma honored Johnny by inviting him to her birthday party. *The Road to Oz,* p. 131. (B)

Johnwan

There was once a wonderful "wozard" in the Gillikin Country. (A wozard is not *quite* as powerful as a wizard.) This particular wozard was named Ozwoz, and he traded one of his wooden soldiers, named Johnwan, to the Red Jinn of Ev for a magic cookie jar that always stayed full, no matter how many cookies were taken from it. Personally, we think Ozwoz got the better of the bargain, but Jinnicky was pleased with his trade. Johnwan is now the personal bodyguard of the Purple Prince of Regalia. *The Purple Prince of Oz*, p. 233. (T)

Jol Jemkiph Soforth

A long time ago, Jol was King of Oogaboo, a tiny country in a desolate corner of Oz. Jol's wife had such a sharp tongue that the poor hen-pecked fellow crept over a mountain pass into Oz proper and has never been heard of since. A few years later, his wife followed. (We hope she didn't find him.) *Tik-Tok of Oz*, p. 14. (B)

Junnenrump

High in the sky over Oz is Stratovania, a land in which all people live out-of-doors under canopies. Junnenrump is the busiest servant boy in that land. Look under any canopy and you'll find him busily fetching and carrying, always ready to jump-en-run for any of the canopy people. *Ozoplaning with the Wizard of Oz*, p. 125 (T)

K is for KINGS—and there is more than one kind, as you have seen. Which would *you* be like— Rinkitink—who was so well loved that he had to scamper off on a vacation for relief? Or like Ruggedo, who was so wicked that he was banished from his own kingdom?

AN "OZ FAN" FRIEND WHOSE NAME BEGINS WITH "K"

One who can laugh, cry, and be merry at the exaggerated antics of kings, and who is here registered as a Citizen of the Land of Oz.

Kabebe

Queen of Stratovania, a country high in the sky, Kabebe behaved like many other high-strung ladies do when their husbands are absent: she tried to run the country. High as it was, Queen Kabebe almost succeeded in running Stratovania into the ground. *Ozoplaning with the Wizard of Oz*, p. 99. (T)

Kabumpo

When Prince Pompadore of the Kingdom of Pumperdink set out to search for his "Proper Princess," Kabumpo the elegant elephant was his faithful companion. Not only is he an elegant elephant; he is an elegant fellow too, and the people of Oz, as well as thousands in the great outside world, are very fond of Kabumpo. *Kabumpo in Oz*, p. 18. (T)

Kachewka

Since he is the Royal Counselor of King Sizzeroo, of Umbrella Island, Kachewka is supposed to do the king's thinking for him. Fortunately for both of them, being king of Umbrella Island is a flighty business and doesn't require much in the way of brains. *Speedy in Oz*, p. 21. (T)

Kalidahs

Dreadful beasts called Kalidahs attacked Dorothy and her friends when they were journeying to the Emerald City on the "road of yellow brick." The sharp wits of the Scarecrow and the sharper axe of the Tin Woodman saved the adventurers from these fierce animals. The Kalidahs have bodies like bears and heads like tigers. Perhaps they got their name from *kaleidoscope,* the pretty toy children love to look into because it shows pictures ever-changing and many-shaped. But we hope none of us ever sees a Kalidah when he looks into the *kaleidoscope! The Wizard of Oz,* p. 58. (B)

Kaliko

When first we heard of Kaliko, he was Chief Steward of the Nome King. Later, when Ruggedo had been banished from his underground kingdom, Kaliko became King of the Nomes. Everyone had thought him a pleasant enough fellow—for a Nome—but, when power was put into his hands, he used it to mistreat the king and queen of Pingaree. Like some folks in the great outside world, Kaliko didn't know how to use success. *Ozma of Oz,* p. 186. (B)

Kangaroo

The only kangaroo in Oz lives just two miles due south of the village of Fuddlecumjig. So, it is only a hop-skip-and-jump for

Kangaroo to reach the village, where old Grandmother Gnit, his friend, sits and g-nits mittens for him, day in and day out—that is, when she isn't scattered over the landscape. *The Emerald City of Oz*, p. 129. (B)

Kapoosa

Kapoosa is the Major Dumbo of Menankypoo in Gnoman's Land, near the Kingdom of Rinkitink. Like all Menankypooians, Kapoosa can't talk. These odd people never speak, but converse by means of words that appear on their foreheads. Maybe this is what people mean when they say they can "read our thoughts." *Pirates in Oz*, p. 27. (T)

Kayub

Gatekeeper of the royal palace of Regalia, in the Gillikin Country, Kayub failed only once in a long career to guard the gate. That was when Kabumpo, the elegant elephant, rumbled in to call on King Randy. Gates and gatekeepers have never bothered Kabumpo, but Kabumpo bothered the gatekeeper! *The Silver Princess in Oz*, p. 23. (T)

Kerr

For a time, Kerr ruled as King of Keretaria, in the Munchkin Country. However, he was a villain and an imposter, and so he couldn't last long in Oz. Handy Mandy gave him a hand down from his throne. *Handy Mandy in Oz*, p. 33. (T)

Kerry

The rightful boy-king of Keretaria, Kerry was a prisoner of the wicked Wizard of Wutz, while Uncle Kerr occupied his throne. Handy Mandy and Nox, the white ox, soon put everything right. Today, King Kerry and Keretaria are as happy as any young king and his country have a right to be—and that's pretty happy in Munchikinland. *Handy Mandy in Oz,* p. 213. (T)

Kettywig

Brother to King Pompus of Pumperdink, in the Gillikin Country, Kettywig is a deep-dyed villain. He once allied himself with the witch, Princess Faleero of Follensby Forest, to steal the throne of Pompus. Kettywig thought he was pretty smart, but he met his match in Faleero, who took over the throne and provided Kettywig with a nice, tight cell in the palace dungeon. When rascals put their heads together, one of them is likely to *lose* his head. Certainly, in this deal, Kettywig didn't get a-head! *The Purple Prince of Oz,* p. 38. (T)

Kik-a-Bray

Dunkiton is a community of donkeys, whose inhabitants declare they are the smartest beings alive. They have no streets in their towns, and their buildings and houses have no numbers. The donkeys believe only stupid people need such guideposts and signs to help them get about. King Kik-a-Bray was so impressed with the good manners and polite words of the Shaggy Man that he gave that unfortunate person a donkey's head, which didn't please Shaggy at all. Kik-a-Bray was much surprised at this for, like all donkeys, he thought no other existence could be so fine. And Shaggy found it very hard to stop being a donkey! *The Road to Oz*, p. 79. (B)

Kiki Aru

At one time, Kiki Aru was a cross, disagreeable, unhappy boy living in Hyup Land on Mount Munch. Then, he learned a secret of transformation, made friends with—of all people!—the Nome King, and caused a great deal of trouble. In order to cure Kiki of his trouble-making, he was forced to drink of the waters of the "Fountain of Forgetfulness", upon doing which he immediately forgot all his wickedness and became a normal, happy youth. *The Magic of Oz*. p. 21. (B)

Kinda Jolly

The King of Kimbaloo, in the Gillikin Country, has exactly five hundred subjects—two hundred and fifty girls and two hundred and fifty boys. Kimbaloo was one of the happiest kingdoms in all Oz until Kinda Jolly made the mistake of hiring Old Mombi the witch as castle cook. What a stew she cooked up! But even that turned out all right, and Kimbaloo is once more one of the merriest kingdoms you can find. *The Lost King of Oz*, p. 13. (T)

King of the Figure Heads

As a king, this one is a dismal disappointment, for the King of the Figure Heads is nothing more than an ordinary school ruler, and he rules the City of Rith Metic. His subjects have thin, wiry bodies on which are mounted, as heads, numerals such as "2", "5", "7", and so forth, up to "10". For all the ruling of their ruler king, the Figure Heads are so stupid that, if they weren't all together looking at one another's heads, not one of them could count up to ten! *Kabumpo in Oz*, p. 66. (T)

King of the Soup Sea

Here is a curious creature made of soup bones, with a cabbage head! He rules happily in a sea of delicious soup, somewhere in the Gillikin Country. *Kabumpo in Oz*, p. 164. (T)

King of the Winged Monkeys

As servant of the Magic Cap, when owned by the Wicked Witch of the West, the King of the Winged Monkeys led his band to capture Dorothy and her companions. Again, when Dorothy possessed the Cap, the Winged Monkeys carried Dorothy and her friends to Glinda the Good, who made it possible for Dorothy to return to Kansas. *The Wizard of Oz*, p. 117. (B)

Kitticut

King Kitticut is the father of Prince Inga of Pingaree, a small but beautiful island noted for its pearl fisheries. Because of the wealth of Pingaree, the island was once attacked by fierce warriors, and King Kitticut and his queen were sold into slavery to the Nome King. Only Prince Inga survived, as you can read in *Rinkitink in Oz*, p. 20. (B)

Kleaver

You've probably seen cleavers in butcher shops, but not live ones, which is what King Kleaver is. He lives in the Kingdom of Utensia, in the Quadling Country. The people of Utensia are all live kitchen utensils: spoons, forks, knives, saucepans, etc. The strangest thing about Utensia is that there is not a cook or a single thing to eat in the whole kingdom! *The Emerald City of Oz*, p. 170. (B)

Kojo

Kojo is a three-legged Tripedalian servant of the friendly little giant, Nandywog, in a valley in the Gillikin Country. Randy and Kabumpo will always remember their visit with Nandywog as one of the more pleasant happenings in *The Purple Prince of Oz*, p. 107. (T)

Konk

King Konk lives on an island in the Nonestic Ocean, where he rules the Shellbacks, an odd kind of people who eat shells. When Peter, Roger the Read Bird, and Cap'n Salt refused to eat with them, Konk flew into a rage and said some "hard" words—in Shell, of course. The three thought they would have to use another kind of shells (ball, shot and bombshell) to "konker" King Konk, but the Shellbacks turned turtle, and our adventurers thankfully turned their backs on the Shellbacks. *Pirates in Oz,* p. 123. (T)

Krewl

Jinxland is really a part of Oz, but it is remotely situated and separated from Oz by a deep chasm. This was a most unhappy land when ruled by King Krewl, and everyone was glad to see him dethroned by the famous Scarecrow, and the beautiful Gloria, the country's rightful ruler, crowned queen in his stead. King Krewl landed another job in Jinxland, where he is now palace gardener. *The Scarecrow of Oz,* p. 140. (B)

Ku-Klip

Surely a greater tinsmith than Ku-Klip never lived, for he made the Tin Woodman of Oz and, later, the Tin Soldier. But when he made the mistake of working in flesh-and-blood (which is certainly no work for a tinsmith) he created Chopfyt, who, if you recall, was "always someone else." *The Tin Woodman of Oz*, p. 216. (B)

Kuma Party

This fellow is able to overcome many problems which trouble us. When Kuma Party wants to go for a walk, he sends his legs out to stretch, and the rest of him stays at home to answer the doorbell. When he wants to attend a concert, he just sends his ears; his eyes, alone, go to the picture gallery. And so it goes—or rather, so goes Kuma Party. He is the son of the remarkable wizard, Wumbo the Wonder Worker. *The Nome King of Oz*, p. 129. (T)

Kumup

Sifting all the facts about Stairway Town, Gillikin Country, we find that it and its king are about the most stupid in all Oz, for subjects and ruler just walk up and down stairs all day long. If only someday one of them would fall downstairs—but nothing *ever* happens! *The Purple Prince of Oz*, p. 96. (T)

Kynd

King Kynd was the father of Princess Gloria, of Jinxland. King Phearce stole the throne from King Kynd, and King Krewl stole it from King Phearce. The Scarecrow gave the throne back to Gloria, who was, by this time, rightful ruler of the realm. *The Scarecrow of Oz*, p. 136. (B)

L is for Love. "The Land of Oz is love," observes Ozma in *Tik Tok of Oz*. This wise ruler knows that love works astonishing wonders and transformations, for love is the most powerful magic of all

AN "OZ FAN" FRIEND WHOSE NAME BEGINS WITH "L".

One who is ever ready to love the good creatures of story who bring so much joy, and who is here registered as a Citizen of the Land of Oz.

Langwidere

When the royal family of Ev was held in captivity by the Nome King, Langwidere ruled in their place. The princess is a very conceited person, with few interests outside her boudoir, where she keeps thirty heads, one for each day of the month. Her room is filled with mirrors, in which Langwidere observes the beauties of her heads. Now that she is no longer bothered with ruling Ev, Langwidere spends all her time changing from a blonde to a brunette to a redhead. (What a find Langwidere would be in Hollywood!) *Ozma of Oz*, p. 88. (B)

Larry

The Lord High Chigglewitz, Chief Personage of the Village of Fuddlecumjig, in the Quadling Country, is known as Larry to his friends. The Fuddles are made up of pieces, like jig-saw puzzles, but they are round, as we are, not flat. They have a habit of "scattering." Once, when Larry scattered himself, he did too energetic a job of it, and a piece of his knee is *still* missing. The old gentleman gets around very well considering that he is nick-kneed! *The Emerald City of Oz*, p. 137. (B)

Laughing Willows

Up in the Gillikin Country, there is a grove of laughing willows. Unlike their cousins, the weeping willows, these willows chuckle all day and all night long. They are not too pleasant, though, for they laugh not *with*, but *at* people. *The Lost King of Oz,* p. 75. (T)

Lazy Quadling

Meet the laziest man in Oz! This Quadling lived beside a river. In order to get him to build a raft, which they needed to cross the river, the Scarecrow and his friends gave Lazy some "square meal tablets". Since the man was too lazy to eat, this was the first square meal he'd had in ages. *The Patchwork Girl of Oz,* p. 306. (B)

Leopard

Right out of the heart of the forest of the Winkie Country comes this leopard to prove, once and for all, that a leopard can and does change his spots—in Oz. Sometimes this leopard's spots are stars; sometimes they are moons; sometimes squares, or oblongs, or triangles—and sometimes—new shapes never before heard of! The leopard was a good friend to Jam, and no matter how furiously his spots changed, his loyalty never did. *The Hidden Valley of Oz,* p. 129. (C)

Li-Mon-Eags

In reality, these two creatures, who existed for only a short time and made much trouble in the Forest of Gugu, were the Nome King and Kiki Aru. Kiki, seeking to impress the forest animals, transformed himself and Ruggedo into animals with the heads of lions, the bodies of monkeys, the wings of eagles, and the tails of wild asses, with knobs of gold on the ends. Never a very straight thinker, Kiki crowned the wrong ends of his animals with gold. *The Magic of Oz*, p. 86. (B)

Little Minty

The village of the Lollies is in the Quadling Country, and Little Minty is one of the coolest and most attractive of its mouth-watering inhabitants. We have heard it said that her first name is *Pepper*. *The Scalawagons of Oz*, p. 34. (N)

Little Pink Bear

The Big Lavendar Bear, King of Bear Center in the Winkie Country, owns the Little Pink Bear, who is not alive. However, when a crank in his side is turned and Little Pink Bear is asked a question concerning the past, he gives an answer that is always truthful (We suppose this might be called getting the "bear" facts!) *The Lost Princess of Oz*, p. 211. (B)

Lonesome Duck

This fanciful fowl, which lives in a diamond castle in the Munchkin Country, has feathers of many colors. Although this bird glories in its lonely life, it came out of seclusion at one time to use the tiny bit of magic it knows to help Trot and Cap'n Bill out of trouble. *The Magic of Oz*, p. 176. (B)

Long-Eared Hearer

Ruggedo, the old Nome King, once had a servant with very long and very sensitive ears. By putting his ears to the ground, this Nome could hear sounds occurring thousands of miles away. Yet when the Hearer caught the sound of the marching feet of the Army of Oogaboo, Ruggedo pulled those ears until it's a wonder they aren't two feet longer. *Tik-Tok of Oz,* p. 104. (B)

Loo

Gugu, ruler of the Forest of Gugu, in the Gillikin Country, has for counselor a unicorn called Loo. When Loo became a man for a short time, he acted in a very foolish manner. Now that he is again a unicorn, he is very much ashamed of the idiotic pranks he played when he had two legs instead of four. *The Magic of Oz,* p. 82. (B)

Lord High Freezer

For the most part, the Winkie Country enjoys the delightful, not too warm temperature which prevails in Oz the year 'round. Still, there is one place in Winkieland called Icetown. The Lord High Freezer is the cold fellow who keeps things iced in Icetown. It is our opinion that the Lord High Freezer needs to be de-frosted. *The Hidden Valley of Oz,* p. 204. (C)

Lord High Humpus

The only important thing Lord High Humpus of Perhaps City (Maybe Mountains, Winkieland) ever did was to rush Prince Tatters into marriage with Princess Pretty Good. We understand that they have a curious marriage ceremony in the Maybe Mountains: when it is time for the groom to say, "I do," he just says, "Maybe." That custom might be very popular with certain people here in the great outside world. *Grampa in Oz,* p. 242. (T)

Lord High Mayor

Not only is the Lord High Mayor very tall, but he lives in Hightown, far up in the air over the Valley of Romance, near the Land of Ev. Up in Hightown, there is absolutely no gravity, although the people are always grave. The Lord High Mayor is sure his town is the world's center of culture and interest. *The Shaggy Man of Oz,* p. 83. (S)

Lord High Upper Dupper

This nobleman held a high place in the Court of Keretaria, in the Munchkin Country. It was his duty to put people in their places. The Lord High Upper Dupper was convinced that the proper place for everyone who didn't agree with him was the Keretaria Klink. *Handy Mandy in Oz,* p. 33. (T)

Lorna

Little is known of Lorna except that she is a wood nymph for whom three strands of emeralds once were made. The emeralds came complete with enchantment. Like so many precious stones, these magic emeralds spelled bad luck for some people, once they had been stolen from Lorna. *The Wishing Horse of Oz*, p. 241. (T)

Loxo

Loxo the Lucky was once a tremendous giant living in the Quadling Country. Today, the tables are turned, and Loxo is no longer a giant; instead, he is just a rather insignificant farmer. *Speedy in Oz*, p. 28. (T)

Lucky Bucky

Lots of small boys go to New York Harbor to see the sights, but we'll wager Lucky Bucky is the only small boy who was ever blown out of a tug boat in that harbor into the Nonestic Ocean! Once there, Lucky Bucky met a wooden whale named Davy Jones and traveled with him to the Emerald City. He liked the adventures he and Davy had on the way to the Emerald City, where he can be found even today. *Lucky Bucky in Oz*, p. 17 (N)

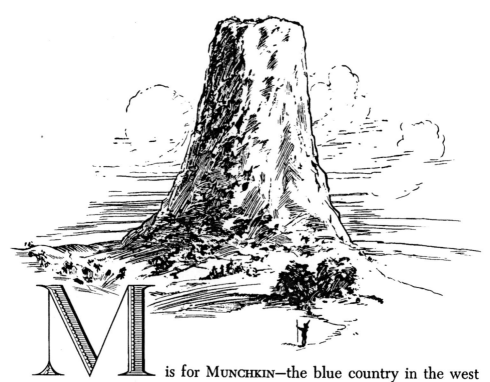

M is for MUNCHKIN—the blue country in the west
and probably the most famous of the four
Oz countries. Dorothy's house landed, you will recall, on
Munchkin land when the powerful
Kansas cyclone carried her to far off Oz

AN "OZ FAN" FRIEND WHOSE NAME BEGINS WITH "M"

One who knows the magic of the enchanted "blue land"
well, and who is here registered as a Citizen of the Land of Oz.

Maltese Majesty

Her Maltese Majesty, the Queen of Catty Corners in the Gillikin Country, rules a village of cats. Each cat's home has a long and comfortable fence around it, just right for midnight concerts. This powerful pussy presides at all the concerts and her voice can be heard above (and below) all the others. Happily, no Gillikin lives within hearing distance of Catty Corners—and that's no accident! *The Lost King of Oz*, p. 86. (T)

Manley, Mrs.

The mother of Jonathon Andrew Manley lives in the State of Ohio with Jam and her professor husband. Since Jam returned from his visit to Oz, Mrs. Manley has been forced to believe that Oz is real, but this is no news to us! We wanted to tell you Jam's Ohio address, but Mrs. Manley asked us not to, until Jam is old enough to answer his own fan mail. *The Hidden Valley of Oz*, p. 18. (C)

Manley, Professor

Jam's father has his laboratory in the big white house in which the family lives in Ohio. The professor does research and uses animals in his experiments, which is how Jam happened to take Percy, the white rat, and Pinny and Gig, the guinea pigs, with him to Oz. It's nice to know that these animals remained in Oz, where they can talk and should have happy lives. *The Hidden Valley of Oz*, p. 21. (C)

Marcia

The Queen of Mudland has just one distinction: She is undoubtedly the homeliest woman in Oz. In fact, she is probably the origin of the expression "ugly as mud." *The Yellow Knight of Oz*, p. 48. (T)

Margolotte

The wife of Dr. Pipt, the "crooked magician," made the Patchwork Girl from an old crazy quilt she found in her attic, and various items from her sewing basket. Poor Margolotte had intended the Patchwork Girl to work as her hired maid, without wages, of course. But, after Ojo gave the girl an overdose of brains, that gaudy maiden had her own ideas about life, and they didn't include being a hired girl for anyone. *The Patchwork Girl of Oz*, p. 26. (B)

Maribella

Maribella is a dainty sky-shepherdess and lives in the clouds over Oz, and over the great outside world, too. She shepherds the stars across the sky every night. Not even the smallest star ever gets lost in the vast expanse of night as Maribella herds them safely across the sky, to make room for the coming day. *Grampa in Oz*, p. 201. (T)

Marygolden

For many years, this little Princess of the Winkie Country was a golden statue. There was very little fun in being a statue, gold or not, so Marygolden was delighted when the Yellow Knight came riding to her rescue and broke the enchantment that had turned her into a statue. She and the Yellow Knight grew so fond of each other that they are now quite happily married. *The Yellow Knight of Oz,* p. 111. (T)

Matiah

If ever there was a scoundrel in Oz, Matiah qualifies for the title. He made people believe he was an honest merchant selling emeralds; but the emeralds were both stolen and enchanted. Then, he posed as a wizard, but he was even more of a humbug than he had been as a merchant. Finally, he wound up as a perfectly ordinary private citizen of Skampavia, and that's letting him off easily, considering all the trouble he caused. *The Wishing Horse of Oz,* p. 38. (T)

Meander

Umbrella Island, a floating bit of earth carried here and there by a magic umbrella, has no telegraph service, but it does possess a royal messenger. His name is Meander. Although the island is not a large one (as sky islands go) it takes a long time for a message to reach its destination. That's because Meander *likes* to meander. *Speedy in Oz,* p. 25. (T)

Memo

This curious little Winkie man never does anything without writing it down on a pad. He has a twin brother named Randum who is just the opposite of thoughtful little Memo. (We have met folks just like both Memo and Randum in our own world.) *The Royal Book of Oz*, p. 186. (T)

Mifkets

Across the Deadly Desert lies the Nonestic Ocean, and on an island in that ocean live the Mifkets. These people once had visitors to their island in the persons of John Dough and Chick the Cherub. They treated John and Chick as mischievously as they did the Scalawagons. The Mifkets and the Scoodlers may be the same people, since they look so much alike. But the Mifkets can't remove their heads, and the Scoodlers can. *The Scalawagons of Oz*, p. 55. (N)

Mira

The Marchioness of Muckengoo, a dismal spot in the otherwise bright Winkie Country, is the sister of Queen Marcia of Mudland. Mira is only a shade better looking than her sister. It seems that any number of mud packs has failed to improve the appearance of these grimy ladies. *The Yellow Knight of Oz*, p. 48. (T)

Mis-erable Mesmerizer

A poor little half-wizard of the Baron Lands, in the Quadling Country, the Mis-erable Mesmerizer should know better than to mess around with magic, but he kept right on meddling and getting into more and more messes. Once, he gave his master a flowing beard—it turned out to be of the kind of whiskers that flow at the rate of six feet per minute! *Jack Pumpkinhead of Oz*, p. 84. (T)

Mist Maidens

The Mist Maidens are about the most attractive creatures you could hope to meet on a hot day in August. They live in a valley in the Gillikin Country, and are lovely and light as gossamer. To see them in their sheltered valley, cool, graceful, and floating, you would think them made of the air itself—and they are. *Glinda of Oz*, p. 53. (B)

Mixtuppa

Mustafa is the Ruler of Mudge, a tiny country in the Munchkin Land, and Mixtuppa is his wife. However, the lady might give you an argument about even that, for she is so confused she isn't sure of anything. Clocks make Mixtuppa furious for, every time she looks one in the face, it shows a different time. Which proves, to her, that clocks are unreliable since they keep changing all the time. *The Cowardly Lion of Oz*, p. 17. (T)

Mo-fi

A curious animal, half monkey and half fish, Mo-fi lives in a sea-forest in the Nonestic Ocean. If you can imagine a monkey that can swim and a fish that can climb trees, that's the Mo-fi. *Captain Salt in Oz*, p. 221. (T)

Mogodore

Known as the Mighty, the Baron of Baffleburg, Quadling Country, the only thing really mighty about Mogodore was his ambition. He actually wanted to conquer Oz and marry Ozma, but he was very quickly put in his place, which was back in his castle. He is content to remain there now, a midget in his tiny kingdom, hoping that some day a nice little Baffleburgundian maiden will come along and consent to mend his socks for him. *Jack Pumpkinhead of Oz*, p. 112. (T)

Mombi

Probably the most famous witch in the Land of Oz, old Mombi played a very large part in the making of Oz history. She guarded the secret of Tip's origin very closely, and it was only when the boy ran away from her that old Mombi got into real trouble. Even then, she did not give up without a struggle, and she fought even the powerful sorceress, Glinda the Good. Glinda finally compelled Mombi to tell the truth about Tip's real identity. You'll be surprised when you find out all about it in *The Land of Oz*, p. 16. (B)

Mooj

A clockmaker named Mooj separated a whole royal family of Oz and caused a great deal of trouble. The King of Seebania became Realbad—a bandit, because of Mooj. His queen, Isomere, mourned her husband and son for years because of Mooj. And Ojo didn't know who his parents were for many years, because of Mooj. As it turned out, Mooj was a better trouble maker than he was clockmaker. *Ojo in Oz*, p. 181. (T)

Moonlight

This lady doesn't live in Oz alone—she lives on high in the heavens, and you can see her almost every night. Hundreds of popular songs and poems have been written about her, and to her. She is a soft and dreamy-eyed damsel who serves Erma, the Queen of Light. *Tik-Tok of Oz*, p. 129. (B)

Mopsi Aru

On the top of Mount Munch, in the Munchkin Country, live the Highups, of which Mopsi is one. In her own country, she is noted for her ability to make very tasty huckleberry pies. She is also famous as the wife of Bini Aru, once a famous sorcerer, and the mother of Kiki Aru, who became involved with the wicked Nome King. *The Magic of Oz*, p. 21. (B)

Muddle

Muddle is a Middling and lives somewhere under the earth in the Land of Oz. These Middlings are most unattractive people, made of mud, twisted roots, and chunks of coal, just as you would expect of those who dwell underground. When the Scarecrow was falling down his family tree, he was stopped by Muddle and the King of the Middlings, who made the stuffed traveler pay a toll before he was allowed to continue his journey. *The Royal Book of Oz*, p. 44. (T)

Mugly

On the fringe of Oz, near the Deadly Desert, live the Headmen, people consisting of nothing but heads. Mugly is one of these folks who cry out whenever a traveler is seen in their land, "Off with his body!" *The Silver Princess in Oz,* p. 69. (T)

Mugwump

General Mugwump is Commander of the Army of the Silver Islands, a realm lying below the surface of the Munchkin Country. The general and his army are famous for their decorations. However, whenever there is trouble, no one can find General Mugwump and his soldiers. But, when the battle has been won by civilians, the general and his army march victoriously in, to receive medals and honors. *The Royal Book of Oz,* p. 114. (T)

Munchkin Farmer

This farmer once made a scarecrow from an old suit of Munchkin clothes and perched him on a pole in a cornfield. Of course, you know what happened after that. *The Royal Book of Oz,* p. 37. (T)

Mustafa

Ruler of the barbarous Kingdom of Mudge, in the southwestern part of the Munchkin Country, Mustafa was once a great lion fancier. He had 9,999 lions, but he wanted one more—the Cowardly Lion of Oz. By the use of trickery and magic, he captured the famous Lion, only to have both him and the other 9,999 lions turn into stone. The Cowardly Lion was finally restored to life, and Mustafa was punished for his evil doing. *The Cowardly Lion of Oz,* p. 15. (T)

N is for NEILL [John R.], celebrated Royal
Artist of Oz. Neill illustrated thirty-five
Oz books, three of which he also wrote. One of the best loved
illustrators of children's books, his drawings
have beauty, lively humor, and charm

AN "OZ FAN" FRIEND WHOSE NAME BEGINS WITH "N"

One for whom the name Neill conjures up a bewildering array of friends from the staidly human to the fantastically absurd, and who is here registered as a Citizen of the Land of Oz.

Nadj

The Queen of Norroway, a tiny island in the Nonestic Ocean, likes nothing better than a fight. The truth is that she has been fighting her neighbors of Roaraway Island for the past three centuries. *Speedy in Oz*, p. 189. (T)

Nanda

This pretty little girl of the Land of Ev is the personal maid of the haughty Princess Langwidere. Many people thought, when Nanda was appointed, that she would be jealous of her mistress, who has thirty heads. But such is not the case, for in Nanda's one head there is a great deal of common sense. *Ozma of Oz*, p. 86. (B)

Nandywog

The "little" giant of the Gillikin Country is one of the friendliest and best-natured giants you'll ever meet. Nandywog is called "little" because he is a mere twenty-four feet tall, and that is short by giant standards. *The Purple Prince of Oz*, p. 103. (T)

Nifflepok

To be a good servant, one must have a good master. Nifflepok was a bad and frightened servant because he worked for the King of the Silver Mountains in the Gillikin Country. If he had worked for someone good and kind, Nifflepok would have been his naturally good-hearted and willing self. *Handy Mandy in Oz*, p. 141. (T)

Nikobo

Here is a hippopotamus who proved to be the best friend a prince ever had. Nikobo of Patripanny Island has a huge body containing a warm heart filled with kindness and affection for Prince Tandy. He now lives in Ozamaland with Tandy. *Captain Salt in Oz*, p. 92. (T)

Nikobob

When Prince Inga of Pingaree conquered Coregos and freed his people from slavery, he sent a charcoal burner named Nikobob back to Pingaree to supervise the rebuilding of the plundered island. So capable was Nikobob that King Kitticut, Inga's father, appointed him Lord High Chancellor. *Rinkitink in Oz*, p. 142. (B)

Nimmie Aimee

A long, long time ago, Nimmie Aimee loved first a woodman, Nick Chopper, and then a soldier, Captain Fyter. But the wicked witch for whom Nimmie worked enchanted the axe and the sword of these two, respectively, so that they cut themselves to pieces. Out of these pieces, Ku Klip, the master tinsmith, made a new man named Chopfyt, named for both the Tin Woodman and the captain. With this misfit combination as her husband, Nimmie Aimee seems to be content. *The Tin Woodman of Oz*, p. 274. (B)

Nina

Until Jinnicky, the Red Jinn of the Land of Ev, came to Nonagon Island, poor Nina, the cat, didn't know what kindness meant. Now she purrs day and night in the comfortable castle of the Red Jinn. *The Silver Princess in Oz,* p. 208. (T)

Nine Tiny Piglets

Once a sailor visited the Island of Teenty-Weent, where everything is very small, and found nine tiny piglets. He took them to Los Angeles and sold them to the Wizard who was performing in a circus. *Dorothy and the Wizard in Oz,* p. 63. (B)

Noma

Beware the Raggle Taggle Gypsy Band! Noma was one of the gypsies who stole Ojo away from his friends. She lured him into one of the gypsy wagons. *Ojo in Oz,* p. 26. (T)

Nome King

Formerly known as Roquat the Red and Roquat of the Rocks, this old Nome, who was once King of all the Nomes, is now called Ruggedo. He has tried on several occasions to conquer Oz, and he once led a horde of vicious creatures through a tunnel under the Deadly Desert to the Emerald City. Now the old Nome King is a wanderer on the face of Oz, all because of his own evil doing. The present King of the Nomes is Kaliko and, while he is not so wicked as the former king, he still slips from good behavior occasionally and has to be straightened out. (*Gnome* is spelled *Nome* in this book because Professor Wugglebug agrees with Mr. Baum, who spelled the word this way.) *Ozma of Oz,* p. 163. (B)

Notta Bit More

Some years ago, Notta Bit More, a jolly clown, was performing in a circus in Stumptown, U.S.A., and selected a little orphan boy from the audience to help him in his act. It was a rainy afternoon, and everyone inside the circus tent felt happy to be inside out of the storm, and so well entertained. Notta recited a bit of verse, saying it would make the orphan boy disappear. It did! He recited it again, and he himself disappeared! Of course there was Oz magic mixed up in that verse, and Notta and Bob Up, the orphan boy, found themselves in Oz. Adventure followed adventure. Now, Notta and Bob Up live in a gaily colored circus tent, just outside the Emerald City, in which they present shows for visitors from all over Oz. *The Cowardly Lion of Oz*, p. 30. (T)

Nox

The Royal Ox of Keretaria, Munchkin, is a magical, snow-white creature, with a most lovable disposition. Nox was a good friend to Handy Mandy when she first came to Oz, and he played a large part in restoring Prince Kerry to the throne. *Handy Mandy in Oz*, p. 29. (T)

Number Nine

This small Munchkin boy was the ninth child in a farm family. He came to the Emerald City to seek his fortune, but he met with bad luck in the form of Jenny Jump. From that time on, Number Nine jumped when Jenny spoke. *The Wonder City of Oz*, p. 48. (N)

O is for OZMA, Princess and Royal Ruler of the Land of Oz. Ozma is, quite possibly, the best-loved ruler known to young people in the world today. Ozma uses all her extensive fairy powers and wisdom to bring happiness to her subjects

---

AN "OZ FAN" FRIEND WHOSE NAME BEGINS WITH "O"

One who has puzzled over the "greatest mystery" in Oz, and who is here registered as a Citizen of the Land of Oz.

Octopuss

Since this pussycat is so-named, has eight legs, and lives on an eight-sided island (in the Nonestic Ocean) she has only eight lives. *Lucky Bucky in Oz*, p. 233. (N)

Og

A long giant with a short name, the less said about Og, the better. This Ogre of Ogowan was shut up in a mountain for five hundred years. *Pirates in Oz*, p. 226. (T)

Ojo

For a long time, no one but Unk Nunkie knew that Ojo was a prince. Ojo's father, the rightful ruler of Seebania, was meanwhile posing as Realbad the bandit. He met Ojo, without knowing the lad was his long-lost son, and the two became real friends, having some fine adventures together. Ojo was used to adventure, for he had had many before he met his father, as you'll discover to your pleasure in *The Patchwork Girl of Oz*, p. 19. (B)

Omby Amby

Omby Amby's flowing green whiskers have been a familiar sight around the Emerald City ever since the Wizard caused that fabulous city to be built. With the coming of Ozma, the "Soldier with the Green Whiskers" was given three appointments: as Guardian of the Gates, as the Royal Army, and as the Royal Police force. *See also*, WANTOWIN. *The Land of Oz*, p. 67. (B)

Opodock

As soon as a magical silver whistle is blown, this enchanted bird answers its summons and blows the whistler anywhere he wants to go. *Ojo in Oz*, p. 84. (T)

Orange Blossom

Although this unattractive lady's name is made to order for weddings, and her brother is King of the Silver Islands, she can't find anyone who will marry her. Once, she had her eye on the Scarecrow, but he escaped. *The Royal Book of Oz*, p. 208. (T)

Orin

One of the loveliest ladies in Oz, Queen Orin of the Ozure Islands is now Queen of the Munchkin Country. With her husband, Cheeriobed, they form a team of the best-loved and happiest rulers in the Land of Oz. *The Giant Horse of Oz*, p. 234. (T)

Ork

The ork of Orkland has wings shaped like inverted chopping bowls, four long, stork-like legs, a parrot-beak and, instead of a tail, a propeller. He once helped Trot and Cap'n Bill and saved the Scarecrow from destruction. *The Scarecrow of Oz*, p. 33. (B)

Orpah

A long time ago, Orpah the merman was captured and held slave of Quiberon, a monster who lurked in the Lost Lake of Orizon, in which the Ozure Isles are located. But the evil sea monster was vanquished, and Orpah now lives happily in Lake Orizon with his fine stable of sea horses. *The Giant Horse of Oz*, p. 94. (T)

Overman-Anu

The champion fighter of the Valley of Voe once was noted far and wide for his bravery in facing the fierce, invisible bears that roam this beautiful valley. One day Overman-Anu climbed the spiral staircase to Pyramid Mountain, leading to the country of the dread Gargoyles. After fighting the Gargoyles nine days, he escaped and returned to Voe. *Dorothy and the Wizard in Oz*, p. 98. (B)

Owl Man

This Phanfasm met General Guph on his way up Mount Phantastico and led that Nome into the presence of the First and Foremost of Phantastico. *The Emerald City of Oz*, p. 118. (B)

Ozana

Once upon a time, long ago, Queen Lurline flew with her fairy band over Oz and saw that it was a most beautiful land, so beautiful that she caused it to become an enchanted fairyland. She left a tiny baby fairy to be its ruler (who, of course, was Ozma). Then she flew over the Deadly Desert to Mount Illuso, where the evil Mimics dwell. There she left one of her fairy band, Princess Ozana, to stand guard against the wicked Magical Mimics, lest they attempt to harm the Oz folk. *The Magical Mimics in Oz,* p. 112. (S)

Ozeerus

A rather unimportant little servant to Silly, the King of Cave City, Ozeerus flashes the "blue flame" on people and thus transforms them into shades and shadows. *The Giant Horse of Oz,* p. 173. (T)

Ozga

The Princess of the Rose Kingdom, near the Land of Ev and the Nome Kingdom, is a distant cousin of Princess Ozma. The Shaggy Man and Betsy Bobbin picked Ozga from the Royal Rose Bush on which she was growing. But the haughty rose subjects refused to recognize her as their ruler, for they wanted a king. Later, Ozga met Private Files of the army of Oogaboo, and they became firm friends. Ozma, realizing it would make them unhappy to be parted, sent them both back to Oogaboo. *Tik-Tok of Oz,* p. 58. (B)

Ozma

Princess Ozma of Oz is one of the most powerful fairy rulers in the world. After being freed from Mombi's enchantment by Glinda the Good, Ozma ruled her country so well that she was loved by all her people. In a time of crisis, when the Nome King built his tunnel under the Deadly Desert and threatened to conquer Oz, the girl ruler refused to fight. Because of her goodness and her faith in right over might, the Nome King was vanquished and his ugly horde of

warriors turned helplessly away. Ozma once made a long and dangerous journey to the country of the Nomes, to rescue the royal family of Ev from slavery. This adventure nearly led to Ozma's own enslavement by the Nome King. Ozma has opened her heart and the Land of Oz to a number of friendless and homeless people from the great outside world. Kindness and love, more than her magical powers, have made Ozma the most dearly-loved of all rulers. *The Land of Oz*, p. 276. (B)

Ozwold

His mate once left Ozwold the Ostrich with a huge egg, from which it was his duty to hatch his son. Ozwold did this with the aid of Scraps, a little boy from Philadelphia, and other companions. Through all the hatching process, Ozwold traveled constantly, his long legs carrying him through some mighty exciting adventures. *The Gnome King of Oz*, p. 190. (T)

Ozwog

The wonderful "wozard" of the Gillikin Country guards his comfortable castle with two thousand huge, wooden soldiers. He commands these wooden-headed soldiers with his "wozardry" (not *quite* so powerful is *wizardry*). *The Purple Prince of Oz*, p. 225. (T)

P is for PRINCE and PRINCESS, of whom both Oz and the great outside world have many. The immortal George MacDonald wrote that *every* boy and girl is born a prince or princess, and loses the title when either one says or does that which no prince or princess would ever say or do.

AN "OZ FAN" FRIEND WHOSE NAME BEGINS WITH "P"

One who hopes always to lay rightful claim to the title "Prince" or "Princess," and who is here registered as a Citizen of the Land of Oz.

Pajonia

The tiny daughter of Prince Pompadore of Pumperdink and his wife Peg Amy, the beloved Pajonia is still too small to have had many adventures, but her mother and father saw some really exciting times in *The Purple Prince of Oz,* p. 22. (T)

Pajuka

When old Mombi was exerting her most wicked magical powers, she enchanted the baby Ozma. At this time, she transformed Pajuka, prime minister to Ozma's father, Pastoria, into a goose. Old Mombi insisted that Pajuka had always been a goose, needing only feathers and a beak, and she confessed she had forgotten what had happened to Pastoria as the result of her evil magic. Pajuka might have been a goose, but he was also a loyal subject. He remained faithful to Pastoria and eventually regained his identity. *The Lost King of Oz,* p. 21. (T)

Palumbo

One of the steadiest men in Oz, Palumbo is the court juggler of the Ozure Islands, Munchkin Country. It is said that he is such a great juggler he can balance even a budget. Since there seems to be no such thing in Oz as money, we wish Palumbo would come into the great outside world, where his talents would really be appreciated. *The Giant Horse of Oz,* p. 22. (T)

Panapee

Another of the royal chamberlains of Oz, Panapee served Mustafa, the Monarch of Mudge, in the Munchkin Country. He got his ruler into real trouble when he put into Mustafa's head the idea of stealing the Cowardly Lion. For, once they had the Lion by the tail, they couldn't let go! *The Cowardly Lion of Oz*, p. 18. (T)

Pansy

Instead of a watch dog, on Umbrella Island they have Pansy, the Royal Watch Cat. Although Umbrella Island wanders all over the wide expanse of the sky, Pansy has never had a "Sirius" fight with the "Dog Star". Her favorite spot in the sky is the Milky Way. *Speedy in Oz*, p. 17. (T)

Panta Loon

The Loons of Loonville, in the Winkie Country, are nothing more than human-sized balloons, inflated with a lighter-than-air gas. Panta and the rest of the Loons live in the tree tops, fastening themselves with cords so they won't float away. Although Panta once captured the Scarecrow, the Tin Woodman, and Woot the Wanderer, he was quick to see the point when Woot showed him a thorn. *The Tin Woodman of Oz*, p. 52. (B)

Para Bruin

Para is a full-size bear made of genuine rubber, with nothing *synthetic* about him. He is the constant companion of John Dough and Chick the Cherub of Hiland and Loland. If you think bouncing a rubber ball is fun, you ought to try bouncing a rubber bear! *The Road to Oz*, p. 222. (B)

Pastoria

This pleasant old gentleman was another victim of Mombi the witch. She enchanted Pastoria and condemned him to live, having forgotten all of his past life, with the Blanks of Blankenburg, under the surface of the Gillikin Country. Poor Pastoria was forced to become a tailor with these strange people who had no visible bodies. However, he was rescued from this fate by Snip, a little Gillikin boy who was also one of Mombi's victims. When Pastoria's memory had been restored and he was revealed as the "lost king" of Oz, he absolutely refused to accept the throne from Ozma, or even share it with her. He wanted only to have a little tailor shop in the Emerald City with Snip, whom he had come to love dearly, as his button boy and faithful assistant. *The Lost King of Oz,* p. 178. (T)

Pat

The Prime Patter of Roganda is a little blue dwarf who lives in Unicorners in the Munchkin Country. What does Pat pat? He pats all the beautiful unicorns, and grooms and cares for them, too. *Ojo in Oz,* p. 230. (T)

Patchwork Girl

Nicknamed Scraps, the famous Patchwork Girl of Oz was made from an old crazy quilt of Margolotte, wife of Dr. Pipt, the Crooked Magician. Just before the Crooked Magician brought Scraps to life, Ojo added more magic brains to her head than Margolotte meant her to have. Margolotte had intended Scraps for her serving girl, but

Scraps had other ideas about that. Instead, she went along with Ojo on a series of exciting adventures, ending in the Emerald City. Here, Scraps became an immediate favorite. Although she may be too boisterous at times, this fault is readily forgiven in the light of her sunny good nature, high spirits, loyalty, and abounding love of life. Not many flesh-and-blood people have as much fun as Scraps, the "crazy quilt" maiden. *The Patchwork Girl of Oz*, p. 35. (B)

Peer Haps

The only time the jolly monarch, King Peer Haps of Perhaps City, atop the Maybe Mountains of the Winkie Country, was ever unhappy was when his Court Prophet stole the beloved Princess Pretty Good. Percy Vere, the forgetful poet laureate of Perhaps City, made a dangerous trip down the mountain to search for the princess. As you well know, Percy Vere persevered through many an odd adventure until he found Princess Pretty Good and made old Peer happy once more. *Grampa in Oz*, p. 96. (T)

Peg Amy

Would you believe that a wooden doll could become the Princess of Sun Top Mountain in the Gillikin Country? It happened! And Peg Amy was the doll's name. It seems a wizard (wicked, of course) named J. Glegg changed Peg Amy into a tree, to avenge himself on her uncle. Cap'n Bill carved a small doll from that tree, and Trot named the doll Peg Amy. Next, the Nome King stole the doll and made it, through his bungling magic, as large as

a person. He also brought the doll to life, but that is just part of the wonderful story of Peg Amy, all of which you can read in *Kabumpo in Oz,* p. 80. (T)

Peggo

Peggo was a swashbuckling pirate who swashed overboard when his legs buckled. He thought he was going to conquer Oz, but he only succeeded in putting his wooden foot in his mouth. *Pirates in Oz,* p. 61. (T)

Pepper and Salt

These are two guards in the Kingdom of Rash, in the Land of Ev. Pepper and Salt feared they might be thrown to the Hungry Tiger, to season Betsy and her friends, who already faced that fate. *The Hungry Tiger of Oz.* p. 77. (T)

Percy

Once an ordinary white rat, doomed to be the victim of experiments in a professor's laboratory, Percy came to Oz with a little boy named Jam. What Oz did for that rat is really worth reading about! Now as big as a human being, he is a very popular member of the animal set of Emerald City. *The Hidden Valley of Oz,* p. 29. (C)

Percy Vere

The court poet and prime favorite of King Peer of Perhaps City invariably forgets the last word of his jingles and rhymes. Percy doesn't exactly write blank verse, he just leaves the last word of his verse blank. But, however forgetful of his rhymes he may be, he never forgets his duty, and he once set out all alone to rescue Princess Pretty Good from a wicked wizard. He found her and made a lot of new friends, too—all the famous Oz folks. *Grampa in Oz,* p. 96. (T)

Pessim

A little old man who lives alone on a small island in the Nonestic Ocean, Pessim is most disagreeable. No one can please him, and he looks on the dark side of every situation, hopefully expecting Oz to come to a terrible end at any moment. When he lived on the mainland of Oz his neighbors found him so unpleasant that they took him off to a deserted island and left him to be a wet blanket all alone. (Perhaps you know some people like him in the great outside world? They are called *pessim*ists.) *The Scarecrow of Oz,* p. 62. (B)

Peter

A little boy from Philadelphia was once carried to Ruggedo Island, in the Nonestic Ocean, by a "balloon bird." This bird planned to take Peter to the sky kingdom of balloons to be an "airrend" boy. Once on the island, Peter met the Nome King, explored a treasure ship, and journeyed to Oz. When he saved the Emerald City from the Nome King, he received an offer from Ozma to become Prince Peter of Oz. But Pete said he'd rather go back to Philadelphia and be a baseball pitcher. There's just one way in which Philadelphia is superior to Emerald City: the City of Love has a large diamond, while the Emerald City has only—well, you finish *that! The Nome King of Oz,* p. 67. (T)

Peter Pun

Once court jester of Corumbia, in the Winkie Country, Peter Pun told too many "punny" jokes and got turned into a funnysuckle vine. The Yellow Knight, having no sense of humor, released him. His fate might well have served as a warning to Professor Wogglebug, but the professor says he knows too many influential wizards *and* wozards in Oz to be frightened! *The Yellow Knight of Oz*, p. 138. (T)

Phearse

Just as bad as his name sounds, Phearse stole the throne of Jinxland from King Kynd. Following this wicked theft, Phearse got himself pushed over a cliff by King Krewl, so that he was no longer in any position to sit on a throne. *The Scarecrow of Oz*, p. 248. (B)

Philador

When we first heard about Philador, Prince of the Ozure Islands in the Munchkin Country, he and all his family were captives of a water monster known as Quiberon. So Philador started out to find help in conquering the wet beast, finding it in the giant horse and succeeding in settling Quiberon's hash once and for all. (In fact, we understand that the Ozure Islands are still dining off Quiberon hash!) Philador is now Prince of the Munchkins. *The Giant Horse of Oz*, p. 29. (T)

Pid

Not a very nice name, for a not very nice person! Pid is one of the Slow Pokes, who live in the Country of Pokes, Munchkin Country. He was once the servant of Sir Hokus of Pokes, now the spirited Yellow Knight of Oz. But Pid was such a slow Poke, he stayed where he was, while the Yellow Knight went on to happier lands and events. *The Royal Book of Oz*, p. 78. (T)

Pigasus

This winged pig lives in the Emerald City and once helped defeat the Nome King, who is still trying to conquer Oz. Pigasus can soar sky high, which might (but doesn't) account for the high cost of pork roasts. Anyone who rides on Pigasus must speak in poetry, for this steed brings out all the ham in his riders. *Pirates in Oz*, p. 190. (T)

Pinny and Gig

These are two of the happiest guinea pigs in Oz. Pinny and Gig escaped from a professor's laboratory and now live in a Munchkin country home, where they are beloved pets. They have recently become good friends of the nine little piglets belonging to the Wizard. *The Hidden Valley of Oz*, p. 29. (C)

Pinny Penny

Being prime minister of Skampavia, a tiny kingdom near the Land of Ev, required great patience and Pinny Penny was greatly relieved when King Skamperoo went away to visit Oz. He was even more delighted when his ruler returned, for the king now no longer behaved like a spoiled child, as he had before he made his historic trip. *The Wishing Horse of Oz,* p. 18. (T)

Planetty

Once a tremendous thunderbolt carried this Princess of Anuther Planet to the Land of Ev. Planetty was made of metal, as are all the people on her planet. She found it a "hard" life and was glad to become the flesh-and-blood Queen of Regalia, wife to King Randy. *The Silver Princess in Oz,* p. 103. (T)

Ploppa

A giant mud turtle named Ploppa lives in a swamp in the Mudland Kingdom of the Winkie Country. You wouldn't expect a turtle to be noted for a good disposition, perhaps, but Ploppa is the one good-natured being in this sticky land of mud. He once helped Sir Hokus escape. *The Yellow Knight of Oz,* p. 39. (T)

Polychrome

The Daughter of the Rainbow lives on the beautiful bow you see arching across the sky following rain. Occasionally, this lovely sky fairy dances off the foot of the rainbow and onto solid earth. On several occasions, she has heedlessly danced on, and her father, the Rainbow King, has lifted his bow without knowing he has left one of his daughters behind. At one such time, Polychrome enjoyed adventures that led to the Land of Oz and the Emerald City. *The Road to Oz*, p. 60. (B)

Pon

There are "from rags to riches" stories in the Land of Oz as well as elsewhere. Pon was once a gardener's boy in the palace of the Kingdom of Jinxland, so poor that he wore rags. Now he sits on a throne, doesn't work at all, and wears only the finest of clothes. *The Scarecrow of Oz*, p. 131. (B)

Pop Lollypop

This lazy fellow just lolls about all day and lets his daughter, Little Minty, clean the house and do all the work. *The Scalawagons of Oz*, p. 35. (N)

Poppet

Poppet is a handsome young doll who faithfully and amusingly serves Princess Ozana of Pineville. You may recall that Pineville is near Cuttenclip Village and the Story Blossom Garden, in the Quadling Country. Many visitors gather here in order to see the many beautiful sights. In fact, it is rumored that Burr Tillstrom once came to Pineville and offered Poppet a contract to go on television. Of course, Poppet would have had to change his name to Puppet, but he thought he preferred to live in the Princess Ozana's land. *The Magical Mimics in Oz,* p. 119. (S)

Postman

The only postman in Oz lives in the Gillikin Country. He has the strange habit of delivering—not letters—but people. Imagine what an incorrect address could do. *The Purple Prince of Oz,* p. 12. (T)

Potaroo

The Royal Wizard of the Nome Kingdom is only a *fifth-rate* wizard. However, he manages to keep King Kaliko amused with such mild magic as flying dinner dishes. (Do you suppose some of these dishes flew too far—clear into the great outside world—where they have become known as flying saucers?) *The Nome King of Oz,* p. 117. (T)

Pozy Pink

This lady's name would make much more sense if it were reversed to Pink Posy. But then, as Shakespeare said, "What's in a name? A rose by any other name would smell as sweet." And who are we to criticize the Queen of Pumperdink? *Kabumpo in Oz,* p. 18 (T)

Preserva

This queen of a strange glass city in the Munchkin Country has gone to too many cooking schools, we fear, for she has preserved all the people in her city. Evidently, her motto is, "Like those whom you can, and those whom you can't like, *can!*" *The Cowardly Lion of Oz,* p. 212. (T)

Prime Piecer

The Prime Piecer does piece work in the Crazy Quilt Kingdom of Patch, in the Winkie Country. He once tried to piece together a plot which would make Scraps, the Patchwork Girl, Queen of the Quilties. But Scrapps soon scrapped with the Piecer, and his plot went to pieces. *The Nome King of Oz,* p. 7. (T)

Prime Preserve

The chief servant of Queen Preserva in the glass city of Munchkinland, where everyone is jellied, preserved, canned and jarred, is not accountable for his actions. The reason for this is that he is pickled. *The Cowardly Lion of Oz,* p. 209. (T)

Prime Pumper

Radio stations have chief announcers, but the Prime Pumper is a chief announcer without a radio station. He chiefly announces distinguished visitors to the royal court of the Kingdom of Pumperdink, which is in the Gillikin Country, *Kabumpo in Oz,* p. 17. (T)

Prince of the Mangaboos

Distinguished by the star he wears, the prince of the inner-earth Kingdom of the Mangaboos took Dorothy and the Wizard to see Gwig, the vegetable sorcerer. These Mangaboos are all as cool as cucumbers. *Dorothy and the Wizard in Oz*, p. 34. (B)

Prince Perix

An unlikely sort of prince, this one! He had a good chance to leap on his white horse and go in search of Princess Pretty Good. Did he go? No, Prince Perix just stayed at home in Perhaps City and let the court poet steal the glory he might have won. Well, it takes all kinds of princes to make a kingdom. *Grampa in Oz*. p. 105. (T)

Prince Pompadore

The royal family of Pumperdink, Gillikin Country, was once threatened with "disappearance" if Prince Pompadore did not marry the "Proper" Fairy Princess. Pompadore and Kabumpo, the elegant elephant, set out in search of such a princess. You can imagine what wondrous adventures they had. *Kabumpo in Oz*, p. 18. (T)

Princess of Monday Mountain

Queen of the Tubbies, together with her large, well-scrubbed daughter, rules over the washerwomen of Monday Mountain, in the Winkie Country. Percy Vere spent one Monday morning in very hot water because the princess wanted to keep him. *Grampa in Oz*, p. 190. (T)

Princess of the Mangaboos

Although Dorothy picked this princess from the plant on which she ripened (the Mangaboos are vegetable people) the wicked princess was as cold-hearted as the rest of her subjects. She had Dorothy and her friends driven into the Black Pit, from which the Mangaboos believed there was no escape. (Of course, there *was!*) *Dorothy and the Wizard in Oz,* p. 59. (B)

Princess Pretty Good

This princess was stolen from her home in Perhaps City by a wicked wizard, who planned to transform her into a lump of earth. But the Princess Pretty Good was *so* good that she became, instead, a lovely flower fairy named Urtha. After many adventures, she is now happily married to Prince Tatters of the Kingdom of Ragbad, in the Quadling Country. *Grampa in Oz,* p. 100. (T)

Private Files

The only private in the army of Queen Ann Soforth of Oogaboo, Private Files handed in his resignation when Queen Ann ordered him to capture Ozga the Rose Princess, Polychrome, and Betsy Bobbin. All Private Files wanted to capture was Ozga's heart, which he did. *Tik-Tok of Oz,* p. 21.(B)

Professor Grunter Swyne

This happy pig is an authority on "cabbage culture" and "corn perfection." Professor Swyne lives with his wife and one child in a tiny cottage in the Munchkin Country. *The Tin Woodman of Oz,* p. 254. (B)

Props

When the theater was in operation in the castle of the Valley of Romance, Lord Props was in charge of the sound effects, stage furniture, etc. He bungled everything badly, but he is doing very well, today, as instructor of the finger painting classes in the College of Arts and Sciences in the Valley of Romance. *The Shaggy Man of Oz,* p. 118. (S)

Pudge

Like many another wise man, Pudge, sage of the country of Ragbad, Quadling Country, is very good at telling other people what to do for the good of their country. Meanwhile, he sits back in an easy chair, awaiting results. *Grampa in Oz,* p. 25. (T)

Puffup

Some folk have a tendency to puff up when they are close to really important personages. This footman in Ozma's royal palace is one of that sort, putting on all sorts of airs because of the people with whom he associates. He really is quite ridiculous as compared with the natural and unaffected Ozzites, such as the Patchwork Girl, the Scarecrow, Dorothy, and Ozma, herself. *Handy Mandy in Oz,* p. 164. (T)

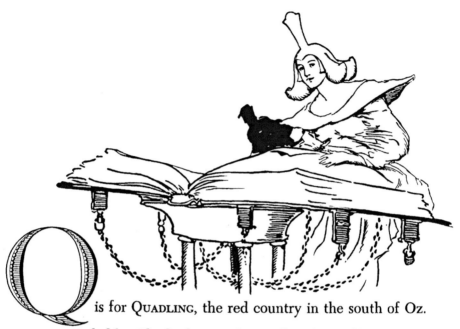

Q is for QUADLING, the red country in the south of Oz. Ruled by Glinda the Good, Quadling has wild, unexplored regions that seem to abound equally in surprising exploits and people. *Quad*ling suggests that it is the fourth of the four countries of Oz

---

AN "OZ FAN" FRIEND WHOSE NAME BEGINS WITH "Q"

One who has known the fun of peeking in upon a war in the Quadling Country, and who is here registered as a Citizen of the Land of Oz.

Quakes

General and Commander of the Pumperdinkian Royal Army, Gillikin Country, Quakes is celebrated for never having lost a battle, which naturally makes him quite a person in Pumperdink. It is considered the worst possible taste to bring up the fact that General Quakes has never *fought* a battle. That, it seems, is a military secret. *Kabumpo in Oz*, p. 27. (T)

Queen of Ev

The Nome King transformed this unfortunate queen into a purple footstool to adorn his chamber of ornaments. What a humiliation for a proud queen to suffer! But Billina, the Yellow Hen, discovered the Nome King's secret—that the entire royal family of Ev were all *purple* ornaments. So Billina had only to look among the thousands of variously colored bric-a-brac to release the royal children from their enchantment. They included five princesses: Evanna, Evrose, Evirene, Evedna, and Evella; and, four princes: Evrok, Evington, Evroland, and Evardo, the eldest, who is the present King of Ev. *Ozma of Oz*, p. 219. (B)

Queen of the Bigwigs

Immense City is in the Nome Kingdom and is inhabited by no one but Bigwigs. Their queen wears the biggest wig of all and is a very proud and overbearing lady. As long as it is daylight, she is nearly 200 feet tall; but, when night falls and she removes her "big wig," she shrinks to a little lady of five-feet-two. The queen is never seen without her wig, although she has very nice brown hair of her own. She also has one little daughter, who is only about 150 feet tall—in the daytime. *The Hungry Tiger of Oz,* p. 208. (T)

Queen of the Field Mice

Mr. Baum really should have found out the name of this delightful character when he wrote about her, for this tiny queen and her subjects twice played an important part in the history of Oz. In *The Wizard of Oz,* the field mice rescued Dorothy, the Cowardly Lion and Toto from the field of deadly poppies, in which they had fallen asleep. In *The Land of Oz,* the Queen of the Field Mice gave the Scarecrow permission to carry a dozen of her little subjects in his straw, to the Emerald City, where he released them. The mice frightened the girl soldier of General Jinjur's Army of Revolt and enabled the Scarecrow to regain his throne. *The Wizard of Oz,* p. 74. (B)

Queen of the Scoodlers

A strange creature rules over the Scoodlers, who inhabit a rocky, barren section of land just across the Deadly Desert from Oz. The Scoodlers have two faces and two sides, and their feet are shaped like the letter "T" turned upside down. They can remove their heads, and, when they find strangers in their land, they throw these heads at the travelers to frighten them away. Once, the Scoodlers captured

Dorothy and her friends and were preparing to make soup of them. Polychrome's cleverness and the fact that the Shaggy Man played baseball when he was a boy saved the group from the Scoodlers' soup kettle. *The Road to Oz*, p. 116. (B)

Quiberon

Quiberon is a fire-breathing, smoke-snorting monster which old Mombi produced from out of her closet. She placed Quiberon in the Lost Lake of Orizon, so that none of the inhabitants of the five Ozure Isles of Oz might ever return to the mainland. The Wizard of Oz quickly tamed Quiberon, and Lake Orizon is no longer smoky. *The Giant Horse of Oz*, p. 20. (T)

Quick Silver

Far below the surface of the Munchkin Country lie the Silver Islands, where Quick Silver is a servant in the royal palace. His hair is silver-white, and he has a queue at least six feet long. Since he is only four feet tall, that is too much queue. Quick Silver is the fastest little man in the Silver Islands. Often, he finds himself returning from an errand while he is still thinking about going! *The Royal Book of Oz*, p. 105. (T)

Quiggeroc

The present general of the armies of the Nome King hasn't been very active for a number of years. Possibly, Quiggeroc thought about the fate of the generals who had preceded him and wisely decided to be seen and heard as little as possible. The Nome

King has a habit of "relieving" his generals when they displease him. Quiggeroc feels fine and doesn't want to be relieved. *Lucky Bucky in Oz,* p. 127. (N)

Quink

Quink, Queen of the Shellbacks, who lives on an island in the Nonestic Ocean, lives on a diet of shells, like all of her subjects. It must be a noisy place at meal time! *Pirates in Oz,* p. 124. (T)

Quox

When this young dragon was only 3,056 years old, he was sent, as an instrument of justice, on an important mission by Tititi-Hoochoo the Great Jinn. Quox was so efficient that, as a result of his mission, the wicked Nome King was deprived of all his magic powers. Ruggedo was forced to leave his underground kingdom and become a homeless wanderer on the face of the earth. At this time, Quox was in great disgrace in his own land. In his youth he had spoken disrespectfully of his famous ancestor, the Original Dragon, the oldest living creature in Oz. *Tik-Tok of Oz,* p. 141. (B)

R is for ROMANCE. Oz romance is the romance of adventure, courage, love, and the magically mysterious. R also stands for REILLY in *Reilly and Lee*, the company which has published the *Oz* books for half a century

AN "OZ FAN" FRIEND WHOSE NAME BEGINS WITH "R"

One who has known the romance of high adventure in the exciting pages of Oz, and who is now a registered Citizen of the Land of Oz.

Ra

Ra is the Queen of the Magical Mimics of Mount Illuso, across the Deadly Desert from Oz. She once led her horde of evil Mimics to the Emerald City in an attempt to conquer Oz and enslave its people. This time, it can be said that Oz was saved by a nose—Toto's nose. The little dog smelled mischief when the Mimics appeared, although no one else suspected anything was wrong. For a very short time, Queen Ra sat on Ozma's throne. *The Magical Mimics in Oz*, p. 41. (S)

Radj

As far as we know, the King of Roaraway Island in the Nonestic Ocean is still engaged in his war with Nadj, Queen of Norroway, a neighboring island. These neighboring islanders have been at war with each other for several hundred years, in a most *unneighborly* fashion. *Speedy in Oz*, p. 191. (T)

Rak

If you're doing crossword puzzles, Rak is the three-lettered name of a monster which flies like an eagle, runs like a deer, and swims like a porpoise. Inside Rak's body—if you're curious—you will find a comfortable furnace of fire. The Rak inhales air but exhales smoke. *Tik-Tok of Oz*, p. 33. (B)

Randum

This small Winkie man does everything without thinking. Randum has a brother named Memo, and we wouldn't be surprised if father was named Paddy Scratch. *The Royal Book of Oz,* p. 187. (T)

Randy

Randy's official name is Randywell Handywell Brandenburg Bompadoo, Prince of the Purple Mountains, on which is perched the Kingdom of Regalia, in the Gillikin Country. Randy was required to prove himself a proper Prince of Regalia. This he did to everyone's satisfaction in *The Purple Prince of Oz,* p. 18. (T)

Rango

This good grey ape lives in the Forest of Gugu in the Gillikin Country. Rango, an elderly ape, quite serious and scholarly, is a counsellor in the court of King Gugu. *The Magic of Oz,* p. 82. (B)

Rattlesnake

Not all like the rattlesnakes we know, this one is as harmless as a baby's rattle. In fact, the Rattlesnake is a great favorite of the Water Babies in the Nonestic Ocean. Once, he and the A-B-Sea Serpent traveled overland to Oz. *The Royal Book of Oz,* p. 30. (T)

Reachard

This long-armed reacher is the right-arm man of the Dictator of Diksey Land, in the Munchkin Country. Reachard has eyes in his finger tips, and his arms are so long they can reach almost anywhere in Oz. We have known some ill-mannered people who reminded us of Reachard—at the dinner table. *Ojo in Oz*, p. 169. (T)

Realbad

Chief of the robber band that roamed the forests of the Munchkin Country, Realbad rescued Ojo from the gypsies who had stolen him from Unk Nunkie. From the moment he saw the boy, Realbad liked Ojo, and was overjoyed when he discovered that Ojo was his long-lost son. And that's not all of the happiness in the story of Ojo. As it turned out, Realbad wasn't really bad—he wasn't even a real bandit! *Ojo in Oz*, p. 48. (T)

Red Kite

Somewhere over Oz, there is a sky-spot to which all the lost kites go. The Red Kite is the leader of these lost kites, and he is the staunch friend of every child who ever lost a kite in the Spring. *The Hidden Valley of Oz*, p. 93. (C)

Reera

This powerful Yookoohoo Witch lives in her secluded cottage in the wild north section of the Gillikin Country. The only real practicing Yookoohoo Witch in Oz, Reera the Red uses her great powers of transformation solely for her own comfort and amusement.

She neither helps nor harms anyone with her magic. Once, she was tricked by a Skeezer boy named Ervic into restoring the three Adepts to their natural shapes. Reera, with great good nature, admitted she had been tricked. Since it had been done in a good cause, she did not regret her action and bore no malice toward Ervic. *Glinda of Oz,* p. 208. (B)

Renard

King Renard the Fourth, known also as King Dox of Foxville, was so pleased with Button Bright that he gave the boy a fox head. Since all the dogs he met barked at him, Button Bright was not at all pleased. Finally, he bathed in the Truth Pond, where everything false vanishes, and his boy head was restored. *The Road to Oz,* p. 40. (B)

Rhomba

Far below the surface of the Winkie Country lies the Kingdom of Subterranea. Here, Rhomba is the chief counsellor of his Imperial Lowness, the Shah. Rhomba speaks low verse in a low voice. In fact, you can't go any lower than Subterranea. *The Yellow Knight of Oz,* p. 96. (T)

Rhyming Dictionary

Joke Book, formerly court jester of Bookville, Winkie Country, was the only "book" who was kind to Dorothy and Jam and their friends. The Rhyming Dictionary helped the travelers escape from Bookville, and then he went to live in the Emerald City. He and Scraps, the Patchwork Girl, are the best of friends; in fact, everyone likes him except Professor Wogglebug, who didn't want me to mention him in this book. Wogglebug is a little stuffy where books are concerned, and he insists that the Rhyming Dictionary is a "popular" or "cheap" edition. Of course, he's popular; but, cheap or not, he has a good heart. *The Hidden Valley of Oz*, p. 156. (C)

Rigmaroles

Inhabitants of a small outlying section of the Quadling Country, the Rigmaroles are incapable of talking directly to the point about anything. When asked a simple question calling for a "yes" or "no" answer, the Rigmaroles launch into a lengthy harangue, making their interrogators wish they'd kept their mouths closed. *The Emerald City of Oz*, p. 232. (B)

Rinkitink

King Rinkitink is a fat, jolly little monarch, who now lives happily in his capitol of Gilgad. At one time, he was most unhappy, since he wanted to enjoy life and see the world, but his people felt that a king's place was in his castle. King Rinkitink escaped and fled to the friendly island of Pingaree (in the Nonestic Ocean). He took with him his talking goat, Bilbil. After a succession of adventures and a pleasant visit in the Emerald City, he was quite content to return to his island kingdom and quietly rule the Rinkitinkers. *Rinkitink in Oz*, p. 32. (B)

Roganda

The Queen of the Unicorns lives in Unicorners in a forest glade in the Munchkin Country. She befriended Ojo and Realbad and was invited to visit the Emerald City. Roganda, who can blow her own horn, was disappointed in the Sawhorse, the only other horse who was in the Emerald City at that time. *Ojo in Oz*, p. 230. (T)

Roger

Roger the Read Bird was the faithful companion of Peter, the boy from America who twice helped to prevent the Nome King from conquering Oz. The Read Bird is good-natured, good-hearted, and he means well; but he is a bit of a bore when you really don't feel like being read to. *Pirates in Oz*, p. 71. (T)

Rollo

The King of the Hoopers is known as Rollo the Worst. The Hoopers live in the wild forest section of the Gillikin Country. They frighten travelers away from their domain by rolling their long, lean bodies into hoops and wheeling furiously toward the startled strangers. *The Lost King of Oz*, p. 71. (T)

Rora

Rora is the wife of Su-Dic, once the ruler of a strange race of people known as the Flatheads, who lived in the Gillikin Country. During the war between the Flatheads and their neighbors, the Skeezers, Rora was transformed into a golden pig by Coo-ee-oh, Queen of the Skeezers. As a golden pig, Rora was just as foolish as she had been as a woman. Seeing that the transformation made no improvement, Glinda the Good changed Rora back into a woman. *Glinda of Oz*, p. 82. (B)

Rosa Merry

This Queen of Kimbaloo, a tiny kingdom in the Gillikin Country, has charge of half the country's five hundred inhabitants. Rosa Merry is responsible for two hundred and fifty girls. Each morning, these girls pick old- and new-fashioned bouquets from Rosa Merry's bouquet bush and distribute them among the nearby Winkie people, who are great flower lovers. King Kinda Jolly has charge of the country's two hundred and fifty boys, who harvest the button crop from Kimbaloo's button woods and distribute buttons to the Winkie housewives, famous as seamstresses. *The Lost King of Oz*, p. 14. (T)

Rough Pasha

The Pasha of Rash is known as Irasha, or the Rough Pasha. To begin with, Rash is a small kingdom in the

Land of Ev. The first thing Irasha did was to steal the throne from the boy prince, Evered. It was several years before Reddy won back his throne. The Rough Pasha was banished to a lonely island. *The Hungry Tiger of Oz,* p. 15. (T)

Roundaboutys

It is as though the Round-aboutys lived their whole lives on one big carousel, as round and round they go. Not overly popular as Oz inhabitants, they stoutly maintain that they move in the best circles. *The Giant Horse of Oz,* p. 190. (T)

Runaway Land

A section of the Winkie Country used to run around the landscape on ten tremendous legs, discovering and claiming people who got in its path. It was a great trial to the map-makers (cartographers, Professor Wogglebug calls them) because they never knew where to locate this section on their maps. One day, the Runaway Land decided it wanted to be an island. On its way to the Nonestic Ocean, it carried Peg Amy, Prince Pompadore, Wag, and Kabumpo across the Deadly Desert to the Land of Ev. Finally, it did become an island in the Nonestic Ocean and was lived on for a number of years by Ruggedo, the former Nome King. *Kabumpo in Oz,* p. 226. (T)

Rusty Ore

Rusty Ore is an ornamental iron worker in the Land of Ev. He once helped Ozma by providing the deflated sky man, Atmos Fere, with a pair of iron shoes, so that he could stay on the ground even when inflated. *The Hungry Tiger of Oz,* p. 191. (T)

S is for SCARECROW. Although stuffed with straw and not
of the human race, the Scarecrow is probably
the most human character in all Oz. He is proud of his brain,
a little boastful, very fond of adventure
or a joke, and is faithful and just at all times

AN "OZ FAN" FRIEND WHOSE NAME BEGINS WITH "S"

One whose story book friends include the one-and-only Scarecrow—man of straw—and who is here registered as a Citizen of the Land of Oz.

Safety Pin Policeman

This minor official does his best to uphold his office and pin down law-offenders in the Winkie Country. But he is only a makeshift, with a copper badge. He tried to pinch Lucky Bucky and Davy Jones, but only succeeded in getting them to see the point. *Lucky Bucky in Oz*, p. 178. (N)

Sally

This salamander came originally from Lavaland Island in the Nonestic Ocean. Sally likes nothing better than to snuggle up and have a nice warm nap in the hot bowl of King Ato's pipe. Maybe Sally is what people mean when they say, "Put that in your pipe and smoke it!" *Captain Salt in Oz*, p. 68. (T)

Salye Soforth

A strange part of this story is that it was not Salye, but her sister, Queen Ann of Oogaboo, who sallied forth to conquer the world. Queen Ann Soforth found this a foolish mission in a world much larger than tiny Oogaboo, and she was soon happy to return to her remote Oz kingdom. Salye had been queening it in Oogaboo while Ann was gone—perhaps that was the reason she had goaded her sister into sallying forth in the first place! *Tik-Tok of Oz*, p. 13. (B)

Samuel Salt

Better known as Captain Salt of Oz, old Sam Salt was once captain of a pirate ship and discovered more adventures than he did gold. After visiting Oz, he reformed and became the official Royal Explorer, finding new countries and claiming them for Oz in Ozma's name. Now, he lives in the Land of Ev and is still having adventures. *Pirates in Oz*, p. 81. (T)

Sandman

Everyone knows the Sandman. Once, the Nome King grew to giant size and carried Ozma's Royal Palace, on top of his head, high into the clouds. Seeing it, the Sandman thought it was some child's dream palace, and so he put all the flesh-and-blood people in it sound asleep. Since he put the Nome King to sleep, too, he did more good than harm. *Kabumpo in Oz*, p. 205. (T)

Santa Claus

The greatly loved and revered patron saint of all children is included in this book because, quite fittingly, he once visited Ozma to attend one of her famous birthday parties. Accompanied by all his Ryls and Nooks, the forest creatures who help Santa fashion all his wonderful toys, Santa Claus was the greatest and most highly honored guest at Ozma's party. *The Road to Oz*, p. 225. (B)

Sawhorse

Early in his adventures with Jack Pumpkinhead, Tip realized that Jack would never be a speedy traveler because of his peculiar construction and the tendency of his joints to bend the wrong way. Tip was eager to get to the Emerald City, so, coming upon a carpenter's sawhorse, he brought it to life with old Mombi's magic Powder of Life. As the first, fleetest, and most famous horse in the Land of Oz, the Sawhorse is the favorite of Princess Ozma, who regards him as her royal steed and has had his wooden legs shod with gold. *The Land of Oz,* p. 47. (B)

Scarecrow

Perhaps the most famous personage in Oz, the Scarecrow was discovered by little Dorothy when the Kansas cyclone first carried her to Oz. Dorothy helped the Scarecrow down from the pole in a cornfield where a Munchkin farmer had placed him, and the straw man accompanied her to the Emerald City. There, after many adventures, the Wizard of Oz filled the Scarecrow's head with a mixture of bran and pins and needles. Since then, the Scarecrow has been one of the wisest men in Oz. His famous brains have solved many knotty problems and helped his friends out of many perilous predicaments. For a short time, the Scarecrow reigned as King of Oz, but he gladly stepped down from that throne when its rightful heiress,

Ozma, appeared to claim it. The Scarecrow now lives in a novel corn-cob castle in the Winkie Country, near the beautiful nickel-plated palace of his bosom friend, Nick Chopper, the Tin Woodman, Emperor of the Winkies. *The Wizard of Oz,* p. 24. (B)

Scarlet Spider

This creature actually threatened the peace of Oz for a short time. But the evil magic which the Mimics had awakened in the Scarlet Spider was not powerful enough to withstand the good magic of the Princess Ozma. *The Magical Mimics in Oz,* p. 175. (S)

Scissor Bird

Ripper, the Scissor Bird, is an important personage in the Winkie Kingdom. Once, the Scissor Bird, who has scissors for a beak, planned to make the Patchwork Girl the Queen of the Quilties of Patch. Scraps had her own ideas about the project, however, and she very quickly scrapped Ripper's plans. *The Gnome King of Oz,* p. 17. (T)

Sevenanone

Together with Sixantwo and Fouranfour, Sevenanone staged a revolution against King Ato of the Octagon Islands in the Nonestic Ocean. They then set out to conquer Oz. But, although all three of them add up to trouble, they don't add up to enough to conquer Oz. Now they are quite content to stay peacably at home on their eight-sided eight islands. *Pirates in Oz,* p. 75. (T)

Sew and Sew

This is the name by which the Queen of Ragbad was once known. That was many years ago, in those trying days when Ragbad was a run-down-at-the-heels kingdom. The queen took off her crown and went to work, becoming plain Mrs. Sew and Sew, seamstress for all the Ragbadians. When prosperity returned to Ragbad, the queen put her crown back on her head and made only the very finest of embroidery. *Grampa in Oz*, p. 15. (T)

Shaggy Man

A long time ago, the Shaggy Man lived in the United States of America. I suppose, in those days, the Shaggy Man was known as a tramp. He had no home, and his clothes were ragged and shaggy. Then he met Dorothy and they journeyed to the Land of Oz together. Both Dorothy and Ozma were so fond of Shaggy that Ozma invited him to make his home in Oz. A natural traveler, Shaggy has explored many strange and unknown corners of Oz during his wanderings. It was he who brought to Oz the famous Love Magnet that hangs over the gates of the Emerald City, so that all who pass through these gates may be loving and loved. *The Road to Oz*, p. 13. (B)

Shagomar

This magnificent deer is the faithful friend of Princess Azarine. Both now live in the Emerald City, and Shagomar has made fast friends of the royal palace animals: Toto, the Cowardly Lion, the Hungry Tiger, and many others. *Ozoplaning with the Wizard of Oz*, p. 199. (T)

Shah

Far below the surface of the Winkie Country is the Kingdom of Subterranea, ruled by his Imperial Lowness, the Shah. This ruler never speaks, because he wants to save his voice, and he wears a mask showing different expressions, to save his face. Oh pshaw, that's enough about the Shah and his subjects! *The Yellow Knight of Oz*, p. 94. (T)

Shampoozle

The Sultan of Suds is the ruler of a tiny kingdom in the Winkie Country. This kingdom and its inhabitants, with the exception of rubber-showerbath and turkish-towel trees—oh yes, and sponge cushions—are made entirely of soap. Scraps, Grumpy, and Peter were once the captives of Shampoozle, but after an unusual adventure, they slipped out of his soapy grasp. *The Nome King of Oz*, p. 178. (T)

Shepherd

The Rolling Country is the most desolate section of all Winkieland. Only one person lives there—a lonely shepherd. You can well imagine the old fellow's puzzlement when, some years ago, he heard a knock on his door. On opening it, his amazement grew! He was greeted by none other than Dorothy and a group of the most celebrated citizens of Oz. The shepherd made them comfortable in his cottage over night, and then gave them valuable information about the country that lay ahead of them. Dorothy noticed a strange thing on this visit—the shepherd had no sheep! *The Lost Princess of Oz*, p. 86. (B)

Shirley Sunshine

This giddy girl has now settled down as the wife of Belfaygor, Baron of the Baron Lands, Quadling Country. At one time, Shirley nearly became the bride of Mogodore. Had she done so, she would have lost the "Sunshine" in her name, for sunshine never penetrates the ugly world in which Mogodore does his perpetual moping. *Jack Pumpkinhead of Oz*, p. 115. (T)

Shoofenwaller

This Nome is Royal Chamberlain of Kaliko, present King of the Nomes, who in turn was once Royal Chamberlain for Ruggedo, the former Nome King. We sincerely hope Oz history doesn't repeat itself as *our* history often does. Imagine—Shoofenwaller, King of the Nomes! *The Wishing Horse of Oz*, p. 188. (T)

Siko Pompous

Siko is a leprechaun from New Jersey. He is very fond of cheese and will grant almost any wish if you reward him with a pound of limburger. He was responsible for Jenny Jump's trip to Oz, and you can be sure the Oz people don't love him for that. Siko just doesn't understand Oz magic and has promised not to meddle any more. *The Wonder City of Oz,* p. 21 (N)

Silly

This King of Silhouettes, the Shadow People of Cave City, just below the surface of the Munchkin Country, would like to reduce everyone to a shadow. Fortunately, his gloomy kingdom has very few visitors. *The Giant Horse of Oz,* p. 172. (T)

Singer of Rash

Here's living proof that it's rash to be a singer if you have a voice like a horse. The Singer of Rash wound up in a dreary place called Down Town, which is reached by subway from the Land of Ev. There he is happily making money singing for the Down Towners, who are so busy making money themselves that they don't have time to stay and listen to his singing, even after they have paid to hear it. This is an ideal situation for the Singer of Rash! *The Hungry Tiger of Oz,* p. 50. (T)

Sister Six

There were so many children in the Munchkin farm family from which Number Nine came that the mother and father despaired of finding names for all of them. So, they just called them by numbers, and Sister Six was the sixth sister. (I wonder, if Sister Six had had a twin brother, whether they would have called him Half-a-Dozen?) *The Wonder City of Oz,* p. 186. (N)

Sizzeroo

The King of Umbrella Island always wanted to travel, but he didn't want to leave his island. That *was* a problem. Waddy, Sizzeroo's Court Magician, cleverly solved this difficulty by building a huge magic umbrella over the island. Immediately, it became a floating island in the sky. After that, Sizzeroo had plenty of adventures and travel, although he has never stepped off his island. (He'd better not, for it's a long step down!) *Speedy in Oz,* p. 17. (T)

Skally

Skally is a member of the robber band of Chief Vaga and his bandits, who lurk in a dark forest in the Quadling Country. Now we're not going to tell you a thing more about Skally; we're just going to make two additions to two words in the sentence before this, and you'll know exactly what to expect when you read about Skally. Ready? Skally*wag* is a member of the robber band of Chief Vaga*bond* and his bandits, who lurk in a dark forest in the Quadling Country. *Grampa in Oz,* p. 51. (T)

Skamperoo

It's wonderful what a trip to Oz can do for some people! Take Skamperoo, the King of Skampavia, for instance: he was once an unhappy and greedy man who made the subjects of his tiny kingdom, near the Land of Ev, most uncomfortable. Then he went to Oz. When he returned to Skampavia, he was good natured, gentle, and a perfect ruler. The Wogglebug takes all the credit for this: he says he put Skamperoo on a diet of Good Government and Municipal Monarchy pills. Personally, I think Skamperoo was just lucky enough to spend one day watching Ozma rule Oz. *The Wishing Horse of Oz,* p. 17. (T)

Skeezers

These people live on an enchanted island in the middle of a deep lake in the far north of the Gillikin Country. There are exactly one hundred and one Skeezers, and they and their island home are noted for strange and surprising magic. They'll bear watching! *Glinda of Oz,* p. 17 (B)

Skippyfoo

Skippyfoo, the Queen of Tappytown, in the Munchkin Country, rules with King Stubby in this strange little kingdom, where everyone is identified and measured by his feet. They don't take finger prints in Tappytown; they take toe prints. Social position and everything else depend on your feet. It's a good place to put your best foot forward. When Realbad, the erstwhile bandit, visited here, he was immediately labeled as a footpad! *Ojo in Oz,* p. 213. (T)

Sky Sweepers

Only once in a while, during the most humid days of summer and again during the storm-brewing days of winter does the sky look as if it needs a good cleaning. That's when the Sky Sweepers come out and start to sweep the rain or snow off the cloud highways, so that they are once more brilliantly blue. *The Wonder City of Oz,* p. 165. (N)

Sky Terrier

Sky Terrier is a little sky puppy who was caught by Bob Up when he was "fishing" in the Sky Land of Un. Bob threw the tiny dog back in the sky so that he could return to his little master, who lived not too far away on one of the smaller child stars. *The Cowardly Lion of Oz,* p. 150. (T)

Slammer

This fellow is right at home where he lives, and maybe you've met his sixteenth cousin where you live. Slammer has a grand time in the Kingdom of Doorways in the Munchkin Country. *The Cowardly Lion of Oz,* p. 78. (T)

Slayrum

Another ringleader in the bandit gang of Realbad, the Robin Hood of Munchkin Forest, is Slayrum. And while we're mentioning Slayrum, we'll round up this whole bandit gang by telling you about Smackemback, too. Alphabetically, Smackemback doesn't belong here, but, since bandits make a business of defying law and order, we don't see how he can object to being slightly misplaced in this book. We understand that, after Realbad gave up banditry, these two had so little imagination and ambition that they settled down to growing purple cabbages in the Gillikin Country. (Well, that's one way to get a-head!) *Ojo in Oz*, p. 52. (T)

Sleeperoo

This great and "snorious" King of the Gapers of Gapers' Gulch, in the Gillikin Country, sleeps for six months and then eats for six months. He is either stuffed or sleepy, and when he isn't the one, then he's the other. No wonder he and his people spend all their time yawning at each other! *The Silver Princes in Oz*, p. 54. (T)

Smerker

The Chief Scorner of Baffleburg in the Quadling Country is an expert at scorning everything and everybody. Smerker has a mechanical lip that rolls back by a crank into a smirk. Here, in the outside world, we know some people who can scorn and smirk just as well as Smerker. They don't have crankable lips to help them, but they are just as cranky as Smerker. *Jack Pumpkinhead of Oz*, p. 140. (T)

Smirch

Smirch is literally a stick-in-the-mud! Like all of the Mudlanders of Mudland in the Winkie Country, Smirch travels around his unattractive country on tall stilts. Even though they have stilts, Smirch and the Miremen don't excite my envy! *The Yellow Knight of Oz*, p. 50. (T)

Smith and Tinker's

Undoubtedly the greatest manufacturing concern in all fairyland, Smith and Tinker's plant is located in the city of Evna, the capitol of the Land of Ev. Here, Smith and Tinker tirelessly turned out such masterpieces of mechanical perfection as Tik-Tok, the machine man, and the mechanical giant with the hammer, who guards one of the mountain passes leading to an entrance to the Nome Kingdom. The original Mr. Smith had acquired the fashionable habit of painting in his spare time. He painted a picture of a river so natural that, as he was reaching across to paint some flowers on the opposite bank, he fell into the water and was drowned. Mr. Tinker invented a ladder so tall that he could rest the end of it on the moon. One night when there was a full moon, Mr. Tinker climbed up his ladder. He found the moon such a lovely place he decided to stay there, so he pulled the ladder up after him—and he has never been seen since! *Ozma of Oz*, p. 55. (B)

Snif

Once there was a ferocious griffin who lost his *grrrr!* He then became a mild-mannered iffin. How Snif the griffin was scared out of his *grrrr!* is a most logical story, for he was held captive for many years in Scare City. A good scare can, sometimes, prove to be a good thing—and this is one of those cases. For this particular iffin became a perfectly delightful adventure-companion for Peter, the boy from Philadelphia. *Jack Pumpkinhead of Oz*, p. 67. (T)

Snip

A long time ago, Snip was one of the Button Boys in King Kinda Jolly's Kingdom of Kimbaloo in the Gillikin Country. Then, Kinda Jolly made the mistake of hiring old Mombi, the witch, as the castle cook. Old Mombi needed a strong young boy to accompany her on her search for Pastoria, the "lost king" of Oz. She chose Snip and abducted him. Adventure followed adventure, and Snip proved his courage by managing to outwit old Mombi and find Pastoria. The old king and the young boy became so fond of each other that they formed a partnership and are now known for maintaining the best tailor service in the Emerald City. *The Lost King of Oz*, p. 20. (T)

Snoctorotomus

A most unpleasant earth serpent that lived in the Munchkin Country bore this serpenty name. He was put away temporarily by Realbad, the bandit. We are grateful to Realbad for dispatching Snoctorotomus, even for a little while. With a name like that, he could be a serious nuisance to readers! *Ojo in Oz*, p. 197. (T)

Snorer

Nickadoodle is Snorer's real name, and sometimes his friends call him Nick—but more often, just Snorer! He is one of the oddest birds you ever met: first of all, he is big—almost as large as a human being—and he snores so loudly that it sounds like a buzz-saw ripping through a tough piece of lumber. Snorer's beak is long and flexible and shaped like a telephone receiver, so that he can curve it back to his ear, hear his own snoring, and thus wake himself. We imagine that Snorer never has to pay his telepone bill. *The Cowardly Lion of Oz*, p. 160. (T)

Snorpus

Once the keeper of the hidden door to the Silver Mountains in the Gillikin Country, Snorpus, the mighty giant, admitted Handy Mandy and Nox into the Silver Mountains. For this grave error, the Wizard of Wutz had him reduced in size and sent him away to be potted. Queen Preserva can explain to you all the niceties of preserving giants. *Handy Mandy in Oz*, p. 122. (T)

Snorpy

Snorpy is on the day shift in vapory Gapers' Gulch in the Gillikin Country. This is the chasm territory where everyone sleeps for six months and then eats away the remaining half of the year. As you might suspect, yawning and gaping is a national pastime. Snorpy failed to sell Kabumpo and party on sharing even so much as a single bite with him, so great was Kabumpo's fear of sliding into the queer habits of Gapers' Gulchers. *The Silver Princess in Oz*, p. 56. (T)

Snufferbux

This poor brown bear suffered five years' of captivity by a gypsy band that roamed through the Munchkin Country. Snufferbux found happiness through meeting Ojo when he, too, became their captive. In the course of making their escape, they both met with breath-taking adventures. Nowadays, honest Snufferbux is just about the happiest bear in Oz; in fact, he is the Royal Bear of the beautiful forest region of Seebania, in the Munchkin Country. *Ojo in Oz*, p. 26. (T)

Soft-Shell Crab

This soft-shell crab didn't make his entrance on toast, with tartar sauce as companion, but we're likely to wish he had. Instead, he came bouncing in upon the scene on the back of a zebra, while Dorothy and her friends were camping in the Quadling Country. His saucy conduct proved sauce enough for all. The friendly zebra brought him forth from his forest pool with the hope of settling an argument, but Mr. Zebra lost the argument and got pinched in the bargain. *The Emerald City of Oz*, p. 159. (B)

Soothsayer

The only fortune teller we know of in the Gillikin Country is the soothayer, who is very good at peering into the future. But he has one trouble: although he peers and he peers, he can't see a thing! In fact, he can't even see things close to him. It was this soothsayer who misdirected Kabumpo and the Purple Prince of the castle of the Red Jinn. *The Purple Prince of Oz*, p. 60. (T)

Sparrow

As a rule, sparrows are not too highly thought of; many people consider the little bird a nuisance. But here is one sparrow whom we can't help admiring, for he tried to set Kiki Aru straight. It happened in the Land of Ev when the sparrow saw Kiki transform himself into a magpie and steal a gold piece from an old man. The sparrow gave Kiki a golden piece of advice about magpies and their habits of stealing from others. *The Magic of Oz*, p. 31. (B)

Speedy

Speedy, a boy who lives in Long Island, New York, with his uncle, once helped his Uncle Billy build a rocket. They had planned to take a trip to Mars, but their plans and their rocket misfired at the same time. Uncle Billy was left behind, and Speedy skyrocketed to Oz. There he met the Yellow Knight and enjoyed some wonderful exploits. When Ozma transported him back to his home, he left his Oz friends with the promise that some day he would return. Speedy kept that promise in another Oz Book called *Speedy in Oz*, The first adventure took place in *The Yellow Knight of Oz*, p. 85. (T)

Spezzle

You've heard of elephant boys, of course. Well, Spezzle is one of them, and his job is taking care of Kabumpo, the elegant elephant of Pumperdink in the Gillikin Country. This is one of the biggest jobs in Oz, but Spezzle likes it. He also likes Kabumpo, and Kabumpo is mighty proud of his little keeper, so everybody's happy. *Kabumpo in Oz,* p. 44. (T)

Spider

There never was a spider as big as this one! There never was a spider as ferocious as this one! He once lived in the deep forest of the Quadling Country, where he preyed on all the animals, large and small. It took no one less than the Cowardly Lion to destroy the evil monster, and the big lion earned the title of King of the Forest for his deed. *The Wizard of Oz,* p. 195. (B)

Spider King

The Spider King is a large purple spider who rules his spider subjects in an obscure nook of the Gillikin Country. The spiders once captured Ozma and Dorothy by weaving soft but strong strands of their webs about the two. A friendly crab who was none too fond of the spiders was glad to oblige Ozma and Dorothy by snipping the strands with his sharp claws, thus freeing the two captives of the Spider King. *Glinda of Oz,* p. 40. (B)

Spikers

Somewhere in the sky over Oz, there is a horde of terrible creatures called "spikers." They look like spiders, except that they are covered with sharp spikes. They attacked one of the Wizard's Ozoplanes, but the ship was too fast for them. The Tin Woodman was pilot of the Ozoplane when this encounter occurred. One of the spikers caught a glimpse of the Tin Man at the controls of the ship and reported in a puzzled fashion to his comrades that he had seen a little tin can rattling around in the big tin can. The Tin Woodman regarded this as an unkind remark. *Ozoplaning with the Wizard of Oz*, p. 76. (T)

Spud

Spud is one of the potato folks of a potato patch in the Quadling Country. Just to put these saucy potato people in their place, we will tell you a little story—a true one, too. Once, a long time ago, there was a society of people who believed potatoes were unhealthful and should not be eaten by human beings. They campaigned against potatoes under the name of "Society for Prevention of Unhealthful Diet." See where Spud got his name? *The Scalawagons of Oz*, p. 207. (N)

Squealina Swyne

Squealina is the wife of Professor Grunter Swyne. With their children, they live in a small cottage near Mount Munch in the Munchkin Country. Being the wife of a professor is sometimes trying, but Mrs. Swyne seems quite content with her lot. *The Tin Woodman of Oz*, p. 253. (B)

Squirrel

This wise little animal lives in the forest surrounding Pineville, on top of a small mountain in the Quadling Country. Once, the squirrel guided Dorothy and the Wizard to the cottage of Princess Ozana. That was when some mighty strange things happened to the Oz people, and Oz was very nearly conquered by *The Magical Mimics in Oz*, p. 102. (S)

Stampedro

The faithful steed of the Yellow Knight, Stampedro was released from enchantment as a chestnut burr by Speedy. As his original self, he had been a handsome chestnut horse, so of course this was the form he returned to after being released from the wicked spell. *The Yellow Knight of Oz*, p. 178. (T)

Stampeero

In Tappy Town, Munchkin Country, Oz, Stampeero is a high official. Like all the Tappy Towners, he reads and talks with his feet. You can tell which of the Tappy Towners are most clever, for they have the largest feet (greater "understanding," you know!) *Ojo in Oz*, p. 207. (T)

Starina

When Jellia Jamb, Ozma's maid-in-waiting, visited Stratovania, high above Oz, King Strut took quite a fancy to her and asked her to remain as Starina of the Realm. That's the same as asking her to become queen. She became Starina for a time, but she found this a nebulous appointment. There is nothing flighty about Jellia, and she got her feet back on solid Oz earth just as quickly as possible. *Ozoplaning with the Wizard of Oz*, p. 95. (T)

Starlight

You've seen this maiden in the sky many times. Shy and retiring, she twinkles at you with a thousand sparkling eyes, warm and friendly in summer, frosty and aloof on cold winter nights. Starlight is one of the light fairies of the court of Erma, Queen of Light. *Tik-Tok of Oz*, p.129. (B)

Sticken Plaster

You would naturally expect to find this individual in the City of Fix, in the Winkie Country. None of the people move about in this strange city, and certainly Sticken Plaster can't move once he has settled down. *The Royal Book of Oz*, p. 170. (T)

Stirem

Of all the many cooks in the Castle Kitchen of Pumperdink (Gillikin Country, Oz) Stirem is by far the most active. He manages to get his lick into every pot, kettle and sauce pan used in the Royal Kitchen. When someone over-eats and medicine is required, Stirem is busy again, stirring the remedy well before it is taken. *Kabumpo in Oz,* p. 15. (T)

Stork

This kindly bird appeared briefly to play an important part in the history of Oz. Very early in his career, the Scarecrow was left clinging to a pole in the middle of a river. Since the Scarecrow cannot swim, he might now be lying at the bottom of that river had not the stork carried him to shore. Of course, the stork didn't mind this at all, for he is used to carrying bundles. *The Wizard of Oz,* p. 68. (B)

Strutoovious

Known as Strutoovious the Seventh, or Strut of the Strat, the haughty King of Stratovania lived in the Stratosphere over Oz. He decided he could conquer Oz easily because it was beneath him. But he was just flying too high, and, instead of conquering Oz, he fell into a heap of trouble with the Ozoplanes. *Ozoplaning with the Wizard of Oz,* p. 82. (T)

Stubby

Stubby, King of Tappy Town, put his foot down when Realbad the bandit danced a clog. It seems that Realbad insulted the king when he danced, for the people of Tappy Town talk by tapping their feet. *Ojo in Oz,* p. 213. (T)

Sultan of Samandra

One of the greatest villains in Oz history, the Sultan of Samandra once conquered his neighboring Winkie Countries, Corumbia and Corabia, and enchanted their rulers and their people. The sultan made the great mistake of telling his magic secrets to his pet dog, Confido. And Confido lived up to his name! *The Yellow Knight of Oz*, p. 63. (T)

Sunlight

This radiantly beautiful maiden serves Erma, Queen of Light. Perhaps Sunlight is the most powerful and important fairy in existence, so far as human beings are concerned. For what would become of all of us without the healthful rays of Sunlight? *Tik-Tok of Oz*, p. 129. (B)

Supreme Dictator

Called the Su-dic for short, this fellow once ruled the Flatheads, occupants of a mountain top in the Gillikin Country. The Su-dic made so much trouble, stealing his subjects' canned brains, working wicked magic, and waging war on his neighbors, the Skeezers, that the Flatheads were glad when Ozma and Glinda conquered him. The three Adepts were appointed to rule in his place. *Glinda of Oz*, p. 74. (B)

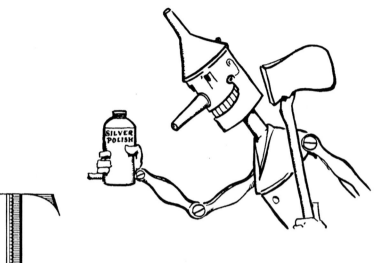

T is for TIN WOODMAN, one of the trio of famous *Oz* characters who were Dorothy's companions on her first visit to Oz. The Scarecrow sought *Wisdom*; the Cowardly Lion, *Courage*; the Tin Woodman, *Kindness*. If each of us found these qualities for himself, what a happy world this would be!

AN "OZ FAN" FRIEND WHOSE NAME BEGINS WITH "T"

One to whom the famous Emperor of the Winkie Country is no stranger, and who is now a registered Citizen of the Land of Oz.

Taka

Taka is the fat chancellor of Menankypoo, located across the Deadly Desert from Oz. The last word we received about Taka was that he and all the Menankypooians had been plundered by pirates, and Taka had been thrown into the sea. For a time Taka stupidly allowed himself to sink, but he found this very uncomfortable, so he started to paddle. This happened a number of years ago, and it may well be that, by this time, Taka will have paddled himself to shore. *Pirates in Oz,* p. 38. (T)

Tandy

Tandy's full name is Tazander Tazah of Ozamaland, which is located on the long continent of Tarara. Boglodore, the Wizard, carried Tandy off into captivity on Patrippany Island. After many exciting encounters, Tandy returned home to Ozamaland and banished his enemies. *Captain Salt in Oz,* p. 107. (T)

Tatters

When Ragbad, a small kingdom in the Quadling Country, was reduced to poverty and King Fumbo lost his head entirely, the handsome young Prince Tatters set out to find a fortune or a wealthy young Princess. With Tatters went Grampa, an old soldier, but not too old to answer his country's call. Tatters and Grampa had some noble adventure which took them through a large part of Oz, during which Tatters found both his fortune and his beautiful young princess, though not just in the manner he expected. Grampa went back to his comfortable rocking chair with enough new stories to satisfy a whole new generation of Ragbadians. *Grampa in Oz,* p. 25. (T)

Tattypoo

Tattypoo thought she was the Good Witch of the North, but she couldn't remember anything about her past life, and her ideas about herself turned out to be a case of mistaken identity. Tattypoo had conquered the Wicked Witch of the North, old Mombi, and the peace-loving Gillikens begged her to rule over them. This she did, using her magical powers to do only good. It was when Tattypoo became curious about her identity that she found out who she really was. *The Giant Horse of Oz,* p. 105. (T)

Tazzywaller

Once the Royal Chamberlain of Mudge in the Munchkin Country, Tazzywaller made a sad mistake by interesting his ruler, the Mustafa, in lions. For Mustafa collected lions, and more lions. When Tazzywaller confessed that he could not possibly add the famous Cowardly Lion of Oz to his king's collection, the poor chamberlain was demoted to feeding the lions. *The Cowardly Lion of Oz,* p. 15. (T)

Teebo

Once upon a time in Ozamaland, there were nine Ozamandarins. These fellows planned to divide Ozamaland into nine parts and rule each separately. Teebo was third in rank among the Ozamandarins, and that meant, by his kind of arithmetic, that he should rule over one-third of Ozamaland. But Prince Tandy appeared on the scene, and you never saw nine madder Ozamandarins. *Captain Salt in Oz*, p. 261. (T)

Terp

This terrible giant once lived in the Hidden Valley of the Gillikin Country. Nowadays that is all in Terp's terrible past. He has become just an average Gillikin farmer and does nothing more terrible than to raise huge heads of purple cabbage. *The Hidden Valley of Oz*, p. 43. (C)

Terrybubble

Once there were huge animals that roamed the earth, larger even than the biggest elephants. Today, all that remains of them is their bones. Scientists wire these bones together and reconstruct the monsters for us to see. Being scientists, they had to give them such difficult names as *dinosaur*. Terrybubble is one of these huge bony creatures who was magically returned to life. He traveled to Oz with Speedy, a boy from Philadelphia. Terrybubble grew very fond of Speedy and proved to be a loyal, if rather large, companion. *Speedy in Oz*, p. 79. (T)

Theodore

The King of the Country of Doorways would naturally have to be named Theo-*dore*. He is terribly hen-pecked by Queen Adora, who wears the keys of the Kingdom of Doorways around her wrist. Theodore can't open a single door without Adora's permission. Unless you enjoy slamming doors, there isn't much reason for you to make a special trip to this little kingdom, so well tucked away in the Munchkin Country that few travelers ever visit it. *The Cowardly Lion of Oz*, p. 81. (T)

Thun

The thunder colt came from "Anuther Planet" on a thunderbolt. When he arrived on earth, he was made of metal and breathed fire. Now, he is a flesh-and-blood horse, and he breathes the good air of Regalia in the Gillikin Country. Thun is a soundless, space-traveling horse who speaks the language of sky writing and belongs to Planetty. *The Silver Princess in Oz*, p. 94. (T)

Thunderbugs

Outside of Oz, these would be plain, ordinary lightning bugs, but in Oz they are wired for sound and are "thunderbugs". These creatures have an Oz-ish craving for raspberry pie, and they give off a light as bright as the lamp in your bedroom. *Lucky Bucky in Oz*, p. 174. (N)

Ticket

King Ticket rules the Valley of Love, formerly known as the Valley of Romance. He is one of the best-loved monarchs outside Oz. The Shaggy Man's Love Magnet is largely responsible for this valley's change of name as well as its inhabitants' change of heart. And the odd part of the story is that the Love Magnet had to be broken before it could bring about this great change in an entire kingdom. *The Shaggy Man of Oz*, p. 112. (S)

Tickley Bender

Of course, you know that every river has a head—it has to have one, because it is a "body" of water! And there is a river in the Nome Kingdom which is no exception. But this river has the head of an old man and is called Tickley Bender. Unlike the "Old Man River" of the song, this Old Man River does "say sumpin"—too much, in fact, for Davy Jones. *Lucky Bucky in Oz*, p. 82. (N)

Tighty

One of the "Out Keepers" of Shutter Town in Winkie Country, Tighty has shutters over his face, like all the weird people of this strange town. When he doesn't want to see a person, he just closes his shutters. We admit this might be a handy arrangement, at times, but we have a feeling it would never be polite. *The Giant Horse of Oz*, p. 214. (T)

Tik-Tok

This extraordinary machine man was made by Smith and Tinker's in the town of Evna, in the Land of Ev. Evoldo, the King of Ev, bought Tik-Tok for a servant. Evoldo enjoyed beating his servants, but Tik-Tok afforded him no pleasure, for the beatings didn't hurt the machine man a bit. Selfish Evoldo then sold his family as slaves to the Nome King, in exchange for a long life. Later he regretted this decision and tried to buy his family back, but the Nome King refused to return them. In despair, Evoldo locked Tik-Tok inside a stone cavern and threw the key into the Nonestic Ocean. He regretted this action, too, jumped in after the key, and was drowned, thus destroying the long life the Nome King had granted him. Dorothy rescued Tik-Tok from the cavern, and he accompanied her to the land of Oz, where he has made his home ever since. In many ways, Tik-Tok, with his clock-work mechanism of pure magic, is much like the electronic robots we read about today. After all, science is nothing more than pure magic, coming true very slowly. *Ozma of Oz*, p. 52. (B)

Til Loon

As Royal Mendress of the Village of Loonville in the Winkie Country, Til Loon gathers up the limp rubber skin when one of the balloon people of that queer town bursts. She mends the puncture and the Loon man or woman can be blown up to proper Loonville size once more. *The Tin Woodman of Oz*, p. 55. (B)

Tin Woodman

A long time ago, Nick Chopper was an ordinary, flesh-and-blood woodman; that is, he dwelt in the forest and chopped down trees for a living. He fell in love with Nimmie Aimee, a young woman who lived with an old witch in the forest. This witch was afraid the hard-working girl would marry and leave her, so she enchanted the woodman's axe. Nick Chopper chopped off an arm. A friendly tinsmith made him a new arm. Then the enchanted axe chopped off his foot, and the tinsmith made him a tin leg. In a short time, he was made entirely of tin, and he was, truly, the Tin Woodman. But the wicked witch had won, for the Tin Woodman had no heart with which to be kind and loving toward Nimmie Aimee. One day he was caught in a rainstorm in the forest and rusted, so that he was no longer able to move. It was thus that Dorothy and the Scarecrow found him. Dorothy oiled his joints, enabling Nick to move about and to talk again. The rest of the Tin Woodman's history is full of adventures, narrow escapes, and happy conclusions. Today he is nickel-plated and lives in a handsome tin palace, where he rules as Emperor of the Winkie Country. *The Wizard of Oz,* p. 37. (B)

Tiny

Tiny is one of the biggest bandits in Realbad's band of forest marauders. In fact, the only thing tiny about Tiny is his intelligence. He has a big appetite, a big ambition, and a big body—but a bean-sized brain. *Ojo in Oz,* p. 48. (T)

Tip

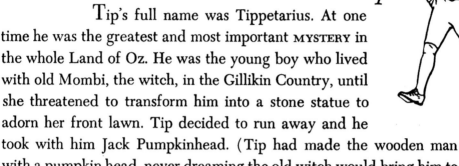

Tip's full name was Tippetarius. At one time he was the greatest and most important MYSTERY in the whole Land of Oz. He was the young boy who lived with old Mombi, the witch, in the Gillikin Country, until she threatened to transform him into a stone statue to adorn her front lawn. Tip decided to run away and he took with him Jack Pumpkinhead. (Tip had made the wooden man with a pumpkin head, never dreaming the old witch would bring him to life.) After many adventures with the Sawhorse, the Scarecrow, and the Tin Woodman, Tip met Glinda, the good sorceress. She immediately knew that Tip was wrapped in some great magical mystery. Only Glinda could solve this. This she did, and from then on Oz was a happier and better land. And Tip was no longer Tip. *The Land of Oz,* p. 7. (B)

Tip Topper

The problem of entertaining visitors is not one which bothers Tip Topper, King of the Topsies of Turn Town, Munchkin Country. The reason for this is that the majority of Oz folk don't like things twisted and turned about as they are in Turn Town, so they just don't visit there. *Handy Mandy in Oz,* p. 79. (T)

Tip Topsy

Queen of Swing City, in the Quadling Country, Tip Topsy has a supurb set of muscles, developed by her habit of swinging from one trapeze to another. She and Hi Swinger, the king, treated Peter and his friends in a very high-handed fashion. *Jack Pumpkinhead of Oz,* p. 180. (T)

Tititi-Hoochoo

Known as the Great Jinjin, Tititi-Hoochoo rules a strange fairyland on the other side of the world from Oz. The Great Jinjin is that country's only private citizen, all his subjects being kings and queens, each wielding great natural powers over mankind. Tititi-Hoochoo is greatly feared and respected for his many awesome powers. His justice is never tempered with mercy. It was he who banished Ruggedo, the Nome King, to the upper earth, to become a homeless wanderer. *Tik-Tok of Oz*, p. 122. (B)

Toddledy

This faithful scribe and Prime Moneyster in the Court of King Cheeriobed of the Azure Islands is a much happier man than he used to be. In the old, bad days, he inscribed in his chronicle many unhappy events brought on by the monster Quiberon. But now that Quiberon is gone, Toddledy's official scribbling is only of gayety and happiness. In fact, his pen fairly dances over the paper now. *The Giant Horse of Oz*, p. 22. (T)

Tollydiggle

The official jailer of the Emerald City is a plump, pleasant, little woman who feeds her prisoners apple dumplings and the most delicious omelettes. That is, she would feed these delicacies to her prisoners except for the fact that, in all her years of service, she has had only one—Ojo, who, when he first came to the Emerald City, made the mistake of picking a four leaf clover. Ojo didn't know this was against the law because four leaf clovers were used by wicked witches and magicians to work evil spells and charms. Of course, Ojo was quickly pardoned by Ozma, but he couldn't say he was sorry he had to spend one night in the Oz jail. Tollydiggle was a much better cook than Unk Nunkie. *The Patchwork Girl of Oz*, p. 196 (B)

Tom

Tom, a young boy from Buffalo, and his twin sister, Twink, started an adventure that led to Oz in one of the strangest fashions you can imagine: They walked through the screen of their father's specially built television set and found themselves on the Isle of Conjo in the Nonestic Ocean. There they met the Shaggy Man, who was on an errand to have the Love Magnet repaired. In no time at all, they were the prisoners of an evil magician, Conjo. From then on, adventures piled one atop the other. *The Shaggy Man of Oz*, p. 13. (S)

Tommy Kwikstep

This young man used to enjoy running errands for people. Once, a witch promised him the fulfillment of one wish if he would run an errand for her. While hurrying on her errand Tommy thoughtlessly said to himself, "I wish I had twenty legs." The next instant, he *had* twenty legs! With such a strangely shaped body, Tommy had to live in a hollow tree. And when his forty feet and two hundred toes developed corns and bunions, Tommy tried unsuccessfully to find the witch who had given him his thoughtless wish, for he no longer enjoyed running errands for anyone. It was Polychrome who kindly used her fairy powers to make Tommy Kwikstep just a quick-stepping, two-legged boy again. *The Tin Woodman of Oz*, p. 135. (B)

Tommy Tallow

One of the Candlemen, who live in the Illumi-Nation, an underground kingdom in the Gillikin Country, Tommy is the most cheerful of these folk, a pretty gloomy lot, living as they do in a land of continual shadows. Tommy once lighted the way for Prince Pompadore and Kabumpo to escape to the upper world of sunlight. *Kabumpo in Oz*, p. 153. (T)

Too Fang

One of the three haughty sons of Chang Wang Woe, Emperor of the Silver Island, Too Fang led his brother in a plot to change the Scarecrow into an ancient Silver Islander. You see, they thought the Scarecrow was their father, the emperor, and if they made an ancient man of the Scarecrow, then they could inherit the throne more quickly. Too Fang soon found out he had bitten off more than he could chew, even with two fangs. *The Royal Book of Oz*, p. 196. (T)

Too Too

Too Too the Second, King and Double King of the City of Double Up in the Winkie Country, is one of the most unpleasant kinglets you will ever meet in Oz. He is really two kings, since everything in Double Up is double. Too Too has two mouths to feed, two necks and four ears to wash and two suits of clothes to press and keep brushed. In addition to all this, Too Too is often of two minds about things—and then his hapless double subjects suffer twice. (We hope you won't find this just too, *too* hard to believe! *The Purple Prince of Oz,* p. 192. (T)

Torpedodo

In Torpedo Town, in the Gillikin Country, everything is very hot, fiery, and explosive. That's why Torpedodo lives there. In his quieter moments, he serves red hot iron rings, which the people of Torpedo Town consider great delicacies, calling them Torpedoughnuts. We understand that Torpedo Town is famous for its hot dogs, too. *The Purple Prince of Oz,* p. 81. (T)

Torpedora

Things are always popping, exploding, banging, zooming and sometimes just fizzling out in Torpedo Town, where Torpedora is Queen. Since Torpedora has the keys to the sulfur-and-brimstone bins, she manages to keep her fire-thirsty subjects in line by threatening to cut down their supply of combustible comestibles. *The Purple Prince of Oz,* p. 80. (T)

Torpy

The chief of the Wakes in Gapers' Gulch in the Gillikin Country bosses the men as they dig the deep pits in which these strange people sleep for six months of the year. Torpy once had a pit dug that was big enough to accommodate Kabumpo, the elegant elephant. But Bumpy had insomnia. *The Silver Princess in Oz,* p. 50. (T)

Toto

Almost everyone who has ever heard of Oz has heard of Toto, Dorothy's little black curly-haired dog, who was her first companion on her first visit to Oz. When Dorothy came to live permanently in Oz, Toto came with her. Since all the Oz animals talk, it finally occurred to Dorothy that it was strange Toto, too, did not learn to speak to her. When Dorothy asked Toto to explain this, the little dog told her—in words—that he and Dorothy understood each other so well there was no need for him to talk. *The Wizard of Oz*, p. 3. (B)

Tottenhots

These strange people live in little underground houses in the Quadling Country. They wear animal skins for clothing and large rings in their ears, for ornaments. While a mischievous lot, the Tottenhots are a harmless people who sleep all day and frolic all night in the moonlight. *The Patchwork Girl of Oz*, p. 243. (B)

Town Crier

In the old days, to "cry the news" was to call it out, loudly, so that all could hear it in the town. Of course, to cry also means "to weep". The Town Crier of Wonder City does both: he cries the news and weeps copious tears, at one and the same time. *The Wonder City of Oz*, p. 87. (N).

Town Crier

Here is a different kind of Town Crier. The people of the City of Kimbaloo, in the Gillikin Country, are so happy that they never cry. Still, they feel that it isn't right to be happy all of the time, so they hire a man who does all their crying for them. *The Lost King of Oz*, p. 41. (T)

Tozzyfog

For two long years, faithful Tozzyfog, of Sun Top Mountain, located in the Gillikin Country, searched for his beloved niece, Peg Amy, not knowing in all this time into what form the princess had been transformed by the wicked magician, J. Glegg. *Kabumpo in Oz*, p. 281. (T)

Trot

Trot and Cap'n Bill lived with Trot's mother in a cottage near the ocean in California. Little Trot Griffiths never grew lonely in the company of the grizzled old sailor, who could spin wonderful yarns of his days on the sea when he was younger and needed no wooden leg. But none of the old man's tales was as wonderful as the adventures they had in Oz. *The Scarecrow of Oz*, p. 13. (B)

Tsing Tsing

This is the wife of Chang Wang Woe, who, a long time ago, was Emperor of the Silver Island, far below the surface of the Munchkin Country. The King of the Golden Islands, who had been defeated in war by Chang, sent a magician to the Silver Island. The magician turned Chang into a crocus. The faithful Tsing Tsing placed that crocus in a bowl. Three days later, the magic crocus had grown into a giant beanpole, its top appearing in a Munchkin farmer's cornfield. According to the magic spell that had been cast, the spirit of Chang Wang Woe would enter the first thing that touched the beanpole. And the first thing that touched the beanpole was—the Scarecrow. *The Royal Book of Oz,* p. 101. (T)

Tubeskins

In the Nome Country, there is a great hollow tube that passes right through the center of the earth. On the other side of the earth, Tubekins is the guardian of that hollow tube. As it is against the law to use the tube for traveling, anyone who zooms out of the tube has to answer to Tubekins, who is also known as the "Peculiar Person". *Tik-Tok of Oz,* p. 112. (B)

Tuzzle

When Tuzzle, Grand Vizier of Samandra, saw his sultan turn a whole kingdom of people into fish, he should have resigned and looked for another job. But he remained in the Sultan's service, who sent him to the Emerald City to bring back the Comfortable Camel. But poor Tuzzle's journey was to no avail. *The Yellow Knight of Oz,* p. 63. (T)

Twiffle

Although he didn't approve of Conjo's magicianship, Twiffle, the little doll-clown, was most loyal to his master. After Conjo drank of the waters of the Fountain of Oblivion, Twiffle went with him back to the Isle of Conjo. He promised Ozma solemnly that he would do his best to see that Conjo used his magic for nothing but good results in the future—with no more stealing of boys and girls from America. *The Shaggy Man of Oz,* p. 18. (S)

Twink

With her twin brother Tom, Twink Jones found her way from Buffalo, New York, to the Emerald City of Oz. Between those two cities occurred some of the most exciting and fascinating adventures you ever read about. *The Shaggy Man of Oz,* p. 13. (S)

Twobyfour

Although Twobyfour was only an unimportant servant to Skamperoo, King of Scampavia, he was responsible, in a way, for the fall of the Emerald City. For it was he who called to the attention of Skamperoo the magic emeralds that came from the Emerald City. Just the sight of those emeralds was enough to make Skamperoo's mouth water. Poor Twobyfour got no reward at all. *The Wishing Horse of Oz,* p. 24. (T)

Twoffle

This small doll-clown lives in the nursery of Twink and Tom Jones in Buffalo, New York. It was Twoffle's cousin, Twiffle, who was partly responsible for the Jones twins' trip to Oz. Now that they are back in Buffalo, Twink and Tom sometimes look long and strangely at Twoffle. Many times, they have resolved to stay up all night and surprise their old friend Twoffle when he makes one of his visits to his cousin in their nursery. But they have never yet been able to stay awake that long. *The Shaggy Man of Oz,* p. 14. (S)

U is for UNITED States. Oz is our contribution to fairyland. Translated into many languages for enjoyment the world over, *Oz* has come to be from America what *Alice* is from England, Grimm's Fairy Tales are from Germany, and the tales of Hans Christian Andersen are from Denmark

---

AN "OZ FAN" FRIEND WHOSE NAME BEGINS WITH "U"

One whose life has been enriched by the great storytellers of *all* lands, and who is here registered as a Citizen of the Land of Oz.

Ugly One

The younger brother of the Shaggy Man was captured by the Nome King and given an ugly face in place of his naturally pleasant one. Ruggedo locked the unfortunate fellow up in a forest in which the trees were made of precious metals and the ground was strewn with valuable jewels. The Shaggy Man heard his brother's plight and set out to rescue him. After a whole "bookful" of adventures the two were reunited. Polychrome, the lovely daughter of the rainbow, broke the Nome King's spell of ugliness by kissing the Ugly One. Shaggy's brother now lives happily in Oz, the guest of Ozma. *Tik-Tok of Oz*, p. 227. (B)

Ugu

When he lived in the City of Herku, Winkie Country, Ugu was a poor shoemaker, very much discontented with his lot. One day, he discovered in his attic a treasure store of magical instruments and books on magic. He stopped making shoes and began the study of magic, with the hope of becoming the greatest magician in Oz, thereby ruling the country. After he became skilled in magical powers, he stole Ozma and enchanted her. On the same night, he also stole all of the important magic in the Land of Oz. And that's how matters stood when Dorothy and her friends set out to search for Ozma in *The Lost Princess of Oz*, p. 241. (B)

Umb

Mount Illuso is a twin mountain in Phantastico, which country borders the Nome Country. The King of the Magical Mimics, who dwell on Mount Illuso, was once goaded by his wife, the evil Queen Ra, into leading his Mimics to Oz, which he very nearly succeeded in conquering. These Mimics are unusual creatures who restlessly change their shapes every few minutes, and they have the power of taking the form of any human being or animal they choose. Even the person mimicked can't tell the difference between himself and his imitator! You can read all about what they did to Dorothy, the Wizard, and other Oz folk in *The Magical Mimics in Oz,* p. 41. (S)

Umph

Like all Nomes, Umph had to try his hand at making trouble, proving to be good at being bad, at least for a time. Eventually, he got his gnarled little fingers burned. *The Wonder City of Oz,* p. 191. (N)

Umtillio

Minstrel in the court of Cheeriobed, King of the lovely and serene Ozure Islands, in the blue Munchkin Country, Umtillio knew a thousand songs, which he sang to please his cheery ruler and the happy people of the islands, playing on his harp to accompany himself. Once upon a time, these islands had been as peaceful as they appeared to be, but the coming of the monster Quiberon ended this serene and happy existence. How Quiberon's noisy tyranny was ended is told in *The Giant Horse of Oz,* p. 22. (T)

Uncle Bill Hugson

Uncle Henry's bother-in-law, Bill Hugson, lives on a large ranch in California. When Dorothy was on her way to the ranch, she, Zeb, and Jim the cab horse fell through a crack in the earth caused by an earthquake, thus embarking on some harrowing adventures. Uncle Bill Hugson was mighty worried and happily welcomed Zeb back when the boy and the old cab horse returned from their incredible experience. *Dorothy and the Wizard in Oz*, p. 17. (B)

Uncle Billy

This kindly inventor lives with his nephew Speedy on Long Island, in New York. They are very fond of each other, and it is for Uncle Billy's sake that Speedy twice has refused to make his home in Oz. *The Yellow Knight of Oz*, p. 85. (T)

Uncle Henry

When Uncle Henry and Aunt Em came to live with Dorothy in the royal palace of the Emerald City, Uncle Henry was not too sure he would be happy amid such splendor, since he had been accustomed to life as a Kansas farmer. However, he found that he could be of help to scores of Ozma's subjects who lived on farms where the soil was not too rich and where crops were difficult to grow. Uncle Henry soon became one of the best-liked celebrities of the Emerald City. *The Wizard of Oz*, p. 2. (B)

Uncles of Wiseacres

They're all here—all the Uncle Georges, Louis, Sams, Bills, Joes, and Zebediahs. Just like uncles outside Oz, they are of all ages, sizes, and dispositions. Uncles are one type of relative who can be almost anything—except aunts. *Lucky Bucky in Oz*, p. 224. (N)

Unk Nunkie

Ojo's uncle was known as Unk Nunkie, the Silent One. And silent he almost *had* to be, for, in the old days, he alone guarded the secret of Ojo's real identity. The Crooked Magician spilled the contents of a bottle of the Liquid of Petrefaction on Unk Nunkie, and the poor old man was silenced completely by being turned into a statue. Only when Ojo met the Wizard of Oz was Unk Nunkie released from the spell. *The Patchwork Girl of Oz*, p. 1. (B).

Urtha   See Princess Pretty Good.

V is for VARIETY, spice of the hectic life lived in Oz.
In wandering through the great lands themselves,
we are first treated to variety in color. In the adventure
we encounter, variety is endless.
And in its formidable *cast of characters,* the variety in Oz leads us
totally out of all the zoos with which we are familiar

AN "OZ FAN" FRIEND WHOSE NAME BEGINS WITH "V"

One on whom the great variety to be found in life is not wasted, and who is here registered as a Citizen of the Land of Oz.

Vaga

When the renegade Vaga captured Prince Tatters of Ragbad, and Grampa, the faithful old soldier, he had to take Bill, the cast iron weathercock from Illinois. Vaga would have enjoyed picking up Bill and casting him back to Illinois on the first "ill wind" that passed by. *Grampa of Oz*, p. 51. (T)

Vanetta

A long time ago, Queen Vanetta of the Blanks was not blank, and neither were her people. They were just ordinary people, ruled by a woman more than ordinarily plain to look at. One day, Vanetta discovered a magic forest pool that rendered invisible those who bathed in its waters. Believing that, if she could not be seen, she would then be thought as beautiful as any maiden, Vanetta took a dip. She was so well pleased with the results of being invisible that she forced all her subjects to plunge in. From that time on, her invisible kingdom was known as Blankenburg, and her people, as Blanks. *The Lost King of Oz*, p. 193. (T)

Vesper Bell

Vesper is one of the Nota-bells who ring in peoples' ears. He accompanied Jenny Jump, with his clear sweet tone, on a notable exploit. *The Scalawagons in Oz*, p. 98. (N)

Victor Columbia Edison

This curiosity is a talking machine (or old-fashioned phonograph) which was accidentally brought to life by Dr. Pipt's Powder of Life. Vic, as Victor Columbia Edison is known, was not at all popular in Oz, perhaps because its records were scratched and its voice even *scratchier*. *The Patchwork Girl of Oz*, p. 57. (B)

Vinegar and Mustard

Vinegar has a sour disposition, and Mustard, a hot temper. That's why these two royal guards of the over-spiced red Kingdom of Rash, in Ev, are so named. *The Hungry Tiger of Oz*, p. 77. (T)

Vig

In a walled city in the Winkie Country live Vig and his subjects. These people of Herku City are served by a race of giants. This is very strange, because Herkus are small and lean, and apparently very frail. Actually, they are the strongest people in the world, from whom their giant servants quail in fear. The Herkus get their strength from Zosozo, a magic liquid invented by Vig. Naturally, the Herkus see to it that not a drop of this strength-giving potion ever passes a giant's lips. But Vig did lend a bottle of it to the Wizard of Oz once, with surprising results. *The Lost Princess of Oz*, p. 168. (B)

Voice That Lost His Man

Once, a singer caught a cold and lost his voice. The Voice was most unhappy and wandered everywhere searching for its master. It spent one evening with Number Nine's family, singing a lullaby to the fourteen children. Everyone concerned was very happy when the Voice finally found his Man and they could sing together once more. *The Wonder City of Oz*, p. 58. (N)

W is for WONDERFUL—the Wonderful Wizard of Oz. It was on that great day many years ago, when the Wizard took his first step out of his balloon onto Oz, that the history of Oz *really* began. Starting out as a humbug, he truly became a *Wonderful Wizard*. With his well known Black Bag of Magic Tools, the little Wizard is loved by everyone who has ever heard of Oz

---

AN "OZ FAN" FRIEND WHOSE NAME BEGINS WITH "W"

One whose excitement at "wizardry" extends to the wizardry of present day scientists, and who is here registered as a Citizen of the Land of Oz.

Waddle

Corporal Waddle, a little brown bear, is the guardian of the entrance to Bear Center, Winkie Country. All the bears who live in that city are stuffed with a fine quality of curled hair and live in comfortable hollow trees. The only creature Corporal Waddle ever succeeded in scaring was a weasel; he shot at it and away it ran. Perhaps the reason for this is that Waddle's sole weapon is a pop gun. *The Lost Princess of Oz*, p. 198. (B)

Waddy

The Wizard of Umbrella Island, which is completely surrounded by air except when it is raining, once came up with a stroke of magic so ingenious it amazed even the Wizard of Oz. Waddy is undoubtedly a wizard just wadded with wonderful magic. *Speedy in Oz*, p. 20. (T)

Wag

This rabbit once lived in the green meadowland just outside the Emerald City. Wag wasn't really a bad bunny, but he got all mixed up with the Nome King, who managed to persuade the baffled bunny to assist in one of the various schemes to conquer Oz. In the course of their plotting, Wag's size increased to ten times that of any normal rabbit. He now lives happily on Sun Top Mountain, where he eats five pounds of carrots a day. *Kabumpo in Oz*, p. 79. (T)

Wagarag

The chief steward to Mogodore, Baron of Baffleburg, Quadling Country, warned his master not to open the "Forbidden Flagon," predicting it's opening would cause great trouble for the Baffleburgundians. At the worst possible moment for Mogodore, the flask *was* opened, and the Baffleburgundians just vanished, but without disappearing. It happened in *Jack Pumpkinhead of Oz*, p. 112. (T)

Wam

The only important magic Wam the wizard ever worked was to enchant three strands of emeralds. He intended them as a gift to Lorna, the wood nymph, from the King of the Green Mountains. But a squirrel stole the emeralds, thinking them green nuts. When he found they were not good to eat, the squirrel discarded the emeralds. Matiah, a Skamperanian peddler, found them—and then the trouble began! *The Wishing Horse of Oz*, p. 283. (T)

Wantowin

This is really Omby Amby, the soldier with the green whiskers. Perhaps the Oz historian who wrote this book wanted to see if you remembered Omby Amby and so invented a new name for him. Well, you did remember, and now Wantowin is again called Omby Amby. *Ozoplaning with the Wizard of Oz*, p. 72. (T)

Weeping Willows

These trees grow on both sides of a river in the Nome Kingdom, weeping real tears into the river. With their long, clinging branches, they push travelers away from the shore. *Lucky Bucky in Oz*, p. 79. (N)

Wheelers

A strange race of people dwell in a rocky section of the Land of Ev. Instead of hands and feet, Wheelers have wheels, with which they roll or wheel themselves wherever they want to go. They are gaudily dressed and, from a distance, give the appearance of human beings with roller skates on both hands and feet. Although they are harmless, the Wheelers are avoided by most folk because of their unfriendly dispositions. *Ozma of Oz*, p. 44. (B)

White Crab

The only white crab we have ever heard of lives in a pool in the Gillikin Country. When he freed Ozma and Dorothy from a magic spider web, by snipping the strands of the web with his sharp claws, Ozma granted him a wish. The crab, green, as all crabs, confessed that he had always longed to be white. Since Ozma's magic is of the whitest white, it was a simple thing for her to make the crab white—and happy. *Glinda of Oz*, p. 43. (B)

White Rabbit

This wise little bunny met Button Bright in a great peach orchard, in the Winkie Country, and warned him that he would have to "answer to Ugu" if he ate a certain peach. That was the first time Button and his friends heard of Ugu, and the knowledge led them straight to *The Lost Princess of Oz*, p. 158. (B)

Wicked Witch of the East

When Dorothy's Kansas home was whisked into the air by a cyclone and settled in Oz, it also settled the fate of the Wicked Witch of the East. She was so bad that no one was sorry to see her destroyed. All that was left of her were the two things which were good—her two shoes, which Dorothy wore in her first journey through Oz. *The Wizard of Oz*, p. 10. (B)

Wicked Witch of the West

Dorothy melted this wicked witch with a bucket of water. The old woman was so dried up and filled with black magic that good clean water melted her down to nothing. By doing this, Dorothy freed herself and the Winkies. *The Wizard of Oz*, p. 110. (B)

Wilby

A woodchopper and a wise man, Wilby refused to become frightened by the Cowardly Lion, and he taught the beast that good will is just as important as courage. The Cowardly Lion learned that sage and friendly words are better, sometimes, than a square meal. *The Cowardly Lion of Oz*, p. 111. (T)

Wiljon

A Winkie farmer named Wiljon was one of the first people to meet the Frogman when he came down the mountain from the secluded Yip country. *The Lost Princess of Oz,* p. 59. (B)

Winks

The Winks guard the passageway to Gapers' Gulch, in the Gillikin Country. (This is one place in which no one ever tried to catch forty Winks!) *The Silver Princess in Oz,* p. 44. (T)

Wizard of Oz

Once, a long time ago, in the great city of Omaha, there lived a happily married politician. Naturally, part of his job as a politician was to kiss many babies. He grew so fond of this part of his work that he decided it would be nice to have a baby of his own to kiss. His good wife thoroughly agreed with him, and so a son, which the politician and his wife considered to be the most wonderful baby in the world, was born to them. So wonderful was this child that the parents sought a remarkable name for him, selecting Oscar Zoroaster Phadrig Isaac Norman Henkel Emmanuel Ambrose Diggs as the lad's impressive cognomen. When the baby grew to be a boy and went to school, he discovered that the initials of all but the first two of this long string of names spelled P-I-N-H-E-A-D.

In desperation, he decided to use only the initials of his first two names, and called himself O. Z. Diggs. When he became a young man, he learned how to do sleight-of-hand tricks and called himself a wizard. To attract people to the circus with which he traveled, he made balloon ascensions, painting his initials (O. Z.) on the side of the balloon. One day, his balloon was caught up by a strong wind and carried to a strange land. When the wizard descended, he was greeted by the local inhabitants as the Wizard of Oz and became their ruler. The rest of his story is so chock full of adventures that the telling of them fills many volumes. On the very spot on which his balloon descended, which happened to be precisely where the four countries of Oz meet, the Wizard ordered built the beautiful and now famous Emerald City. *The Wizard of Oz,* p. 97. (B)

Wizard of Wutz

This is a very minor wizard who once aspired to be the ruler of Oz. Thanks to Handy Mandy and Himself, the elf, Wutz is now one of the prickliest cactus plants anyone ever backed into. *Handy Mandy in Oz,* p. 132. (T)

Wogglebug

"I started life as a lowly bug in the fields of the Winkie Country. It was a wretched existence, for I had to live in continual fear of the great birds who ate helpless insects. Since I didn't know how to make clothing for

myself, I shivered in the cold and sweltered in the heat. One happy day, I crawled, exhausted, into a little red building, which I was to learn later was a school house; there, I made my home between two of the warm hearth bricks. I paid close attention to Professor Nowitall as he taught the children, and I thus acquired a very complete education. One day, the professor discovered me crawling over the hearth. That was my moment of great destiny, for he placed me in a machine which projected me, in a magnified state, onto a screen. Of course, I stepped from the screen as Professor H. M. Wogglebug, T.E. (The letters *H.M.* stand for Highly Magnified; *T. E.*, for Thoroughly Educated.) I am now Dean of the Royal College of Oz and the most learned and important educator in the favored Land of Oz."

The above was written for this book by Professor Wogglebug, himself. We found it so well written that we have made no changes, other than to take the bugs out of the spelling. For a first reference to Professor Wogglebug, see *The Land of Oz*, p. 142. (B)

Woodchopper

This friendly woodcutter once knew the Tin Woodman when he was a flesh-and-blood person. Again, when Ojo started with Unk Nunkie on his first adventure in Oz, it was this woodchopper who gave him some very helpful information about the Land of Oz. *The Patchwork Girl of Oz*, p. 74. (B)

Wooden Gardener

One of the small wooden folk fashioned by the fairy Princess Ozana was a wooden gardener, who cared for the Story Blossom Garden in the Village of Pineville. Since then, he has been promoted and is now in charge of conducting visitors through the garden. *The Magical Mimics in Oz,* p. 134. (S)

Woot

Woot the Wanderer lives in the Gillikin country, but he is seldom at home. He once wandered into the Tin Woodman's nickel-plated palace in the Winkie country and started Nick Chopper on the most important quest of his career. Although we haven't heard about Woot for a long time, we presume he is still wandering. *The Tin Woodman of Oz,* p. 14. (B)

Woozy

The body of this curious animal is shaped like the building blocks with which children play. Its head is likewise block-shaped, and its tail and legs are short and stubby. Once, the Woozy believed it had a terrible growl that would frighten the most ferocious beast, but it found, to its chagrin, that the only beast frightened by that growl was—the Woozy! It does have one real talent, though; when it is angry, its eyes flash real fire! *The Patchwork Girl of Oz*, p. 102. (B)

Wumbo

A crystal cavern in the Kingdom of Zamagoochie, Gillikin Country, is the home of Wumbo, the Wonder Worker. Wumbo works magic solely for his own amusement, and he is a happy and contented little man. Magic and contentment seem to run in Wumbo's family, for his son is the wise and wondrously dis-jointed Kuma Party. *The Nome King of Oz*, p. 227. (T)

X is for Kiss. X has but one *really* important function in the English language, and that is to line up in rows at the close of letters. Kisses express all degrees of endearment, in Oz; consequently, "X" is a hard-working character indeed

---

AN "OZ FAN" FRIEND WHOSE NAME BEGINS WITH "X"

A rare mortal to be sure, whose name begins with "X," is proudly registered here as a Citizen of the Land of Oz.

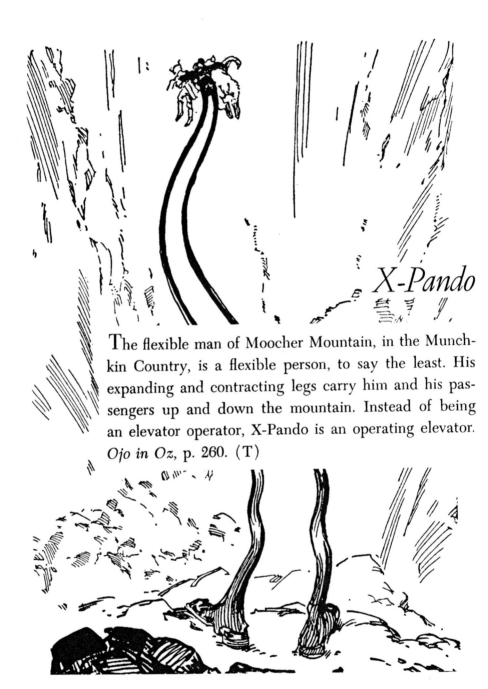

X-Pando

The flexible man of Moocher Mountain, in the Munchkin Country, is a flexible person, to say the least. His expanding and contracting legs carry him and his passengers up and down the mountain. Instead of being an elevator operator, X-Pando is an operating elevator. *Ojo in Oz,* p. 260. (T)

Y is for You, for without you there could be no Land of
Oz. Your appreciation has made Oz *live*
in a very special way, but no less truly than anything else
that draws breath in our great and
mysterious world

AN "OZ FAN" FRIEND WHOSE NAME BEGINS WITH "Y"

You who have signed your good name on yonder line
are here declared to be a registered Citizen of the Land of Oz.

Yellow Hen

This barnyard fowl is the most valuable resident of the City of Perhaps, in the Maybe Mountains. Instead of being an egg layer, as might be expected, Yellow Hen is a brick layer. And, since she is yellow, the hen naturally lays gold bricks. You can imagine how convenient this is for the treasurer of Perhaps City. (Please don't confuse this character with Dorothy's yellow hen, Billina.) *Grampa in Oz*, p. 104. (B)

Yoop

Yoop is the largest untamed giant in captivity. When last measured, he stood twenty-one feet tall in his stocking feet. He is now imprisoned in a cage. *The Patchwork Girl of Oz*, p. 258. (B)

Yoop, Mrs.

For many years now, the giant Yoop has been confined in a cage in the Quadling Country. During all that time, Mrs. Yoop has lived in a huge castle in the Winkie Country. She was a Kookoohoo, which means she was an artist in transformations and could change the shape of anyone or anything. In addition, she was one of the cleverest all-around magic workers in Oz. She wisely kept to herself and her magic harmed no one. But she was selfish, never lifting a finger to free her captive husband. Eventually, she came out of seclusion and used her powers wickedly to change Woot into a green monkey. Since her power was so great, Ozma couldn't change Woot's shape, so she just changed the green monkey into Mrs. Yoop, and Woot became himself. *The Tin Woodman of Oz*, p. 70. (B)

Z is for oZ—last instead of first—a rare and adventurous letter. *Zee*, which is *zed*, which is *izzard* (you'll note its presence in *wizard*), also makes a bold appearance in such time-tested favorites as *The Prisoner of Zenda, The Mark of Zorro*, and *Prince Zalinski's Secret*. In *Rupert of Hentzau* and *Tarzan of the Apes*, its appearance is somewhat more stealthy

---
AN "OZ FAN" FRIEND WHOSE NAME BEGINS WITH "Z"

A rare and elusive bird is Z———, whose name, signed at the appointed place above, attests to registration as a Citizen of the Land of Oz.

Zeb Hugson

Zeb's uncle, Bill Hugson, married Dorothy's Aunt Em's sister, so that made Zeb Dorothy's second cousin. Working as a hired boy on the Hugson ranch, Zeb hitched Jim, the cab horse, to the buggy and drove to the Hugson's Siding railroad stop. Here he met Dorothy, who was coming to visit her Uncle Bill Hugson. On the way back to the ranch there was a terrible earthquake, and the buggy, Zeb, Dorothy, Eureka (the kitten) and the cab horse dropped through a crack in the earth. During the adventures which followed, Zeb proved brave and cheerful. When the travelers finally found their way to the Emerald City of Oz, Dorothy had become so fond of Zeb that she was very sorry to see him return to the ranch. (There are many people living today who remember that California earthquake and what it did to San Francisco.) *Dorothy and the Wizard in Oz*, p. 15. (B)

Zebra

Zebra lives in a forest in the Quadling Country. Like others of his species, he has refused to allow man to domesticate him, although he is closely related to the horse. This particular zebra trotted into the camp of Dorothy and her friends one night and asked them to settle an argument between him and a soft-shell crab. (See SOFT SHELL CRAB.) *The Emerald City of Oz*, p. 158. (B)

Zella

Nikobob, once a charcoal burner on the island of Regos, brought his daughter Zella a pair of shoes which he had found in a trash can in the rear of the royal palace. Neither Zella nor Nikobob knew that those shoes contained two of the magical pearls which were Prince Inga's source of power. The happy conclusion found Zella living on the island of Pingaree, where her father is now King Kitticut's prime minister. *Rinkitink in Oz,* p. 143. (B)

Zerons

These flaky Zerons live on an exceedingly cold mountain in the Nome Kingdom. They have the power to make it cold for anyone who visits their mountain. It's a law there that anything above zero must be lowered immediately. *Lucky Bucky in Oz,* p. 66. (N)

Zinaro

The wife of Zithero, leader of a gypsy band, doesn't have music even in her name, as her husband does. Zinaro spent most of her time telling peoples' fortunes and cooking up a hot, peppery stew. It was she who enticed Ojo into the gypsy encampment. *Ojo in Oz,* p. 45. (T)

Zithero

Here he is, obediently next to his wife—Zithero—leader of the Gypsy band that stole Ojo away from his Unk Nunkie. Zithero is not really a bad sort, but being a gypsy leader, he feels that he simply must live *down* to his reputation. Realbad the bandit caught him up short. *Ojo in Oz,* p. 39. (T)

Zixi

Queen Zixi of the fairyland of Ix appears to be about sixteen years of age, but she has, in reality, lived for many thousands of years, for she knows the secret of remaining forever young and beautiful. She is the firm friend of King Bud and Princess Fluff, whose Kingdom of Noland adjoins hers. *The Road to Oz,* p. 235. (B)

Zunda

And now a lowly inhabitant of Subterranea, a gloomy city far below the surface of the Winkie Country, attains the prominence of being our last hero. Happily, Zunda *did* do something remarkable once—remarkable for a Subterranean, that is. He reflected a glimmering of sunlight when he befriended Speedy, the small boy who was trying to escape from the underground kingdom, as you will learn in *The Yellow Knight of Oz,* p. 99. (T)

Appendices

Story Highlights of the Thirty-Nine Oz Books Published from 1900 to 1951

The Wizard of Oz

[Originally published as *The Wonderful Wizard of Oz*]

It is in this book that Oz is "discovered." A little Kansas girl—Dorothy Gale—is carried in her house to Oz when a cyclone whisks it through the sky. As the house lands in the Munchkin Country (one of the four great countries of Oz) it destroys a wicked witch and sends Dorothy off on her first adventure in Oz. She finds the Scarecrow, meets the Tin Woodman and the Cowardly Lion, melts a second wicked witch with a pail of water and finds her way home. Since this book appeared a half-century ago, we have learned many marvelous things about the Land of Oz. BAUM [L. FRANK] and DENSLOW [W. W.] 1900. (The current edition is illustrated by Evelyn Copelman.)

The Land of Oz

[Originally published as *The Marvelous Land of Oz*]

This sequel to *The Wizard of Oz* deals entirely with the early history of Oz. No one from the United States or any other part of the "great outside world" appears in it. It takes its readers on a series of incredible adventures with Tip, a small boy who runs away from old Mombi, the witch, taking with him Jack Pumpkinhead and the wooden Saw-Horse. The Scarecrow is King of the Emerald City until he, Tip, Jack, and the Tin Woodman are forced to flee the royal palace when it is invaded by General Jinjur and her army of rebelling girls. *The Land of Oz* ends with an amazing surprise, and from that moment on Ozma is princess of all Oz. BAUM and NEILL [JOHN R.] 1904.

Ozma of Oz

Few of the Oz books are as crowded with exciting Oz happenings as this one. Not only does it bring Dorothy back to Oz on her second visit, but it introduces Dorothy to Ozma, relates Ozma's first important adventure, and introduces for the first time such famous Oz characters as Tik-Tok, the mechanical man, Billina the hen, the Hungry Tiger, and—*the Nome King!* Most of the adventures in this book take place outside Oz, in the Land of Ev and the Nome Kingdom. Scarcely a page fails to quiver with excitement, magic and adventure. BAUM and NEILL, 1907.

Dorothy and the Wizard in Oz

Of course, everyone always predicted it would happen! And in this book it does—the Wizard comes back to Oz to stay. Best of all, he comes with Dorothy, who is having adventure number three that leads her to Oz, this time via a California earthquake. In this book we meet Dorothy's pink kitten, Eureka, whose manners need adjusting badly, and two good friends who we are sorry did not remain in Oz—Jim the cabhorse, and Zeb, Dorothy's young cousin, who works on a ranch as a hired boy. BAUM and NEILL, 1908.

The Road to Oz

We like to think of this volume as "The Party Book of Oz." Almost everyone loves a party, and when Ozma has a birthday party with notables from every part of fairyland attending—well! It is just like attending Ozma's party in person. You meet the famous of Oz, and lots of others, such as Queen Zixi of Ix, John Dough, Chick the Cherub, the Queen of Merryland, Para Bruin the rubber bear and—best of all—Santa Claus himself! Of course there are lots of adventures on that famous road to Oz before the party, during which Dorothy, on her way to Oz for the fourth time, meets such heart-warming characters as the Shaggy Man, Button-Bright, and lovely Polychrome, daughter of the rainbow. BAUM and NEILL, 1909.

The Emerald City of Oz

Here is a "double" story of Oz. While Dorothy, her Aunt Em and Uncle Henry experience the events that lead to their going to Oz to make their home in the Emerald City, the wicked Nome King is plotting to conquer Oz and enslave its people. Later we go with Dorothy and her friends in the Red Wagon on a grand tour of Oz that is simply packed with excitement and events. While this transpires, we learn also of the Nome King's elaborate preparations to conquer Oz. As Dorothy and her friends return to the Emerald City, the Nome King and his hordes of warriors are about to invade it. How Oz is saved is an ending that will amaze and delight you. BAUM and NEILL, 1910.

The Patchwork Girl of Oz

Here, the Patchwork Girl is brought to life by Dr. Pipt's magic Powder of Life. From that moment on the action never slows down in this exciting book. It tells of Ojo's quest for the strange ingredients necessary to brew a magic liquid that will release his Unk Nunkie from a spell—the spell cast by the Liquid of Petrefaction, which has turned him into a marble statue. In addition to the Patchwork Girl, Ojo and Unk Nunkie, this book introduces those famous Oz creatures, the Woozy, and Bungle the glass cat. Oz certainly has become a merrier, happier land since the Patchwork Girl came to life, and this is the book that tells how Scraps came to be made, how she was brought to life, and all about her early adventures. BAUM and NEILL, 1913.

Tik-Tok of Oz

For the second time a little girl from the United States comes to Oz. Betsy Bobbin is shipwrecked in the Nonestic Ocean with her friend Hank the mule. The two drift to shore in the Rose Kingdom on a fragment of wreckage. Betsy meets the Shaggy Man and accompanies him to the Nome Kingdom, where Shaggy hopes to release his brother, a prisoner of the Nome King. On their way to the Nome Kingdom, one fascinating adventure follows another. They meet Queen Ann Soforth of Oogaboo and her army, and lovely Polychrome, who had lost her rainbow again; they rescue Tik-Tok from a well; and are dropped through a Hollow Tube to the other side of the world where they meet Quox, the dragon. You'll find it one of the most exciting of all the Oz books. BAUM and NEILL, 1914.

The Scarecrow of Oz

This is the Oz book which L. Frank Baum considered his best. It starts quietly enough with Trot and Cap'n Bill rowing along a shore of the Pacific Ocean to visit one of the many caves near their home on the California coast. Suddenly, a mighty whirlpool engulfs them. The old sailorman and the little girl are miraculously saved and regain consciousness to find themselves in a sea cavern. (To this day, Trot asserts she felt mermaid arms about her during those terrible moments under water.) From here on, one perilous adventure crowds in upon another. In Jinxland they meet the Scarecrow who takes charge of things once Cap'n Bill is transformed into a tiny grasshopper with a wooden leg. An exciting royal reception greets the adventurers upon their return to the Emerald City. BAUM and NEILL, 1915.

Rinkitink in Oz

Prince Inga of Pingaree is the boy hero of this fine story of peril-filled adventure in the islands of the Nonestic Ocean. King Rinkitink provides comic relief, and by the time you reach the final page you will love this fat, jolly little king. Bilbil the goat, with his surly disposition, provides a fine contrast to Rinkitink's merriment and Prince Inga's bravery and courage in the face of danger. Some may say that the three magic pearls are the real heroes of this story, but the pearls would have been of little use to King Kitticut and Queen Garee if Prince Inga hadn't used them wisely and courageously. BAUM and NEILL, 1916.

The Lost Princess of Oz

Talk about *Button-Bright* getting lost—*Ozma* is almost as bad! This is actually the second time Ozma has been lost. As you know, once she was "lost" for many years. But in this book she is lost for only a short time. As soon as it is discovered that the ruler of Oz is lost—and with her all the important magical instruments in Oz—search parties, one for each of the four countries of Oz, set out to find her. We follow the adventures of the party headed by Dorothy and the Wizard, who explore unknown parts of the Winkie Country in search of Ozma. How Ozma is found, and where she has been, will surprise you. Frogman, a new character, is introduced in this book. BAUM and NEILL, 1917.

The Tin Woodman of Oz

Woot the Wanderer causes this chapter of Oz history to transpire. When Woot wanders into the splendid tin castle of Nick Chopper, the Tin Woodman and Emperor of the Winkies, he meets the Scarecrow, who is visiting his old friend. The Tin Woodman tells Woot the story of how he had once been a flesh-and-blood woodman in love with a maiden named Nimmie Aimee. Woot suggests that since the Tin Woodman now has a kind and loving heart, it is his duty to find Nimmie Aimee and make her Empress of the Winkies. The Scarecrow agrees, so the three set off to search for the girl. No less surprising than the adventures encountered on the journey is Nimmie Aimee's reception of her former suitor. BAUM and NEILL, 1918.

The Magic of Oz

Old Ruggedo, the former Nome King, comes to Oz for the second time, and makes more trouble than he did on his first visit. Ruggedo never gives up the idea of conquering Oz, and this time he has the advantage of being in the country without Ozma's knowledge. Also, he has the magic and somewhat grudging help of Kiki Aru, the Munchkin boy who is illegally practicing the art. If you like magic, then this is a book for you. There's magic on every page, and everyone in the story eventually is transformed into something else, or bewitched in one way or another. Even the wild animals in the great Forest of Gugu do not escape. BAUM and NEILL, 1919.

Glinda of Oz

This is the last Oz book written by L. Frank Baum. It is one of the best in the series, with Dorothy, Ozma, and Glinda in an adventure that takes them to an amazing crystal-domed city on an enchanted island. This island is situated in a lake in the Gillikin Country. Ozma and Glinda are confronted by powerful magic and determined enemies. For a time Dorothy and Ozma are prisoners in the crystal-domed city which is able to submerge below the surface of the lake. Few of the Oz books equal this one in suspense and mystery, but it has less humor than some of the other books, perhaps because Mr. Baum was ill while writing it. BAUM and NEILL, 1920.

The Royal Book of Oz

This is the first Oz book written by Ruth Plumly Thompson, who was but twenty years old when she wrote it. Professor Wogglebug lets fall the weighty observation that the Scarecrow has no background—no family tree. So the Scarecrow indignantly goes in search of his family tree to the Munchkin corn field, where he had been placed on a pole long ago to frighten away crows. The pole turns out to be a magic bean pole, and the Scarecrow falls down it, far below the surface of Oz, down to the Silver Islands. Here, the Scarecrow discovers that he is supposed to be the re-created Emperor Chang Wang Woe of the Silver Islands. Among the new characters introduced are: Sir Hokus of Pokes, Comfortable Camel, and Doubtful Dromedary. THOMPSON [RUTH PLUMLY] and NEILL, 1921.

Kabumpo in Oz

This is the first Oz book with an animal in its title role. Kabumpo, however, is much more than an animal—he is a genuine personality. Kabumpo the elegant elephant is the wisest and oldest living creature in Pumperdink.

The excitement begins in this book when the royal family of Pumperdink—King Pompus, Queen Posy, and Prince Pompadore—are threatened with "disappearance" unless the prince marries a "Proper" Princess. Peg-Amy, a live wooden doll, Wag the rabbit, the Nome King, and J. Glegg and his Mixed Magic are all mixed up in Prince Pompadore's search for the Proper Princess. THOMPSON and NEILL, 1922.

The Cowardly Lion of Oz

The Mustafa of Mudge collects—of all things—lions! And he is very unhappy because he is convinced that no really worthwhile lion collection can be complete without at least the tail of the Cowardly Lion of Oz. He makes his big mistake when he sets out to collect the Cowardly Lion, for the Lion has become one of Dorothy's constant companions and is just about the most important animal in Oz. After a bookful of startling adventures, the monarch of Mudge winds up with a collection of stone lions and an enormous and ugly statue filling his courtyard. You'll enjoy meeting Notta Bit More the clown, and his friend Bob Up, in this book. THOMPSON and NEILL, 1923.

Grampa in Oz

The Kingdom of Ragbad is in pretty bad shape. The Queen does the sewing and mending for her people—there aren't any new clothes—and the King has lost his head, *really* lost his head. That is how things are when Grampa, the old soldier, steps forward and declares that something must be done. And Grampa *does* it. With Prince Tatters he starts out in search of the king's head, a fortune, and a princess for Prince Tatters. They find all three, and each in the most miraculous manner. There's a new character in this book of whom you will be very fond. He's Bill the, cast-iron weathercock. THOMPSON and NEILL, 1924.

The Lost King of Oz

What happened to Pastoria, King of Oz in the old days, long before the Wizard came to Oz and erected the Emerald City? That question has been asked many times. Long an Oz mystery, this book settles the matter at last. You won't be surprised to learn that Mombi, the witch, is involved. Also entangled in Pastoria's history are Snip the lovable little button boy, Pajuka the goose who is also a Prime Minister, and Humpy, a Hollywood dummy. Once freed of Mombi's enchantment, Pastoria proves to be a delightful old man who has not the slightest desire to be king of anything. He is perfectly happy with his little tailor shop and his assistant, Snip the button boy. THOMPSON and NEILL, 1925.

The Hungry Tiger of Oz

Everyone knows that the Hungry Tiger of Oz is the largest, the most powerful, and the most magnificent tiger in existence. Realizing this, can you imagine a "little" girl so huge in size that she fondles the Hungry Tiger as though he were a kitten, dressing him in doll clothes like a baby? That's what happens to the Hungry Tiger in this book. Maybe it's punishment for his pretended desire to eat a fat little baby. Reddy, the young Prince of Rash, wins back his kingdom, Ozma is taken sky riding by a gigantic airman named Atmos Fere, and the Nome King concocts more mischief. You'll like Carter Green the vegetable man, who makes his first appearance here. THOMPSON and NEILL, 1926.

The Gnome King of Oz

This is Peter's first visit to Oz—Peter being a small boy from Philadelphia—and he manages to make it an exciting one. Peter accompanies the Nome° King on another of that former monarch's periodic attempts to conquer Oz. While this is happening, the Quilties of Patch are trying hard to make the Patchwork Girl their queen. Scraps objects violently, for the cross-patch life of the Queen of the Quilties doesn't appeal to jolly Scraps. Peter and Scraps meet for a breathless series of adventures. Peter arrives in the Emerald City just in time to save the city from the Nome King. Ozma offers to make him a prince of Oz. Peter, however, prefers his dream of Peter on the pitcher's mound back home in Philadelphia, to a throne in the Emerald City. THOMPSON and NEILL, 1927.

°Also spelled Gnome in Oz books.

The Giant Horse of Oz

This is the third horse in all the Land of Oz. The first is the wooden Saw-Horse, who looks only vaguely like a real horse, but is nonetheless Ozma's favorite steed. The second is Jim, an old cab horse now retired to pasture on a California ranch. Jim doesn't stay long in Oz—magic makes him nervous. High Boy, the giant horse of Oz, is one of the most remarkable creatures you will ever meet. He has expanding and contracting legs, so that he can adjust them to mountains or plains and speed along with equal ease. Highboy races through some remarkable adventures in this book with Prince Philador, Benny the "public benefactor" and many other fascinating Oz folk. THOMPSON and NEILL, 1928.

Jack Pumpkinhead of Oz

Jack Pumpkinhead, who claims no less a personage than Ozma as his royal "parent", makes his own book here, and it's one that should win Jack many thousands of new friends. We meet another old friend in this story: Peter, the little Philadelphia boy, is back in Oz again, and he and Jack have some wonderful times together. They meet the Iffin, who is as charming a creature as you ever saw. They also meet mad Mogodore the robber baron, who actually captured Ozma and believed he was on his way to becoming King of Oz. He was on his way all right—and you'll see how. THOMPSON and NEILL, 1929.

The Yellow Knight of Oz

Sir Hokus, once of Merrie England but more recently of Pokes City, Oz, is always ready for a new exploit. He relishes nothing more than the slaying of a herd of dragons or the rescuing of a bevy of beautiful princesses.

The Yellow Knight, Sir Hokus, has enough adventures to satisfy the most ambitious of knights. He not only rescues a fair princess, but he frees two whole kingdoms of hundreds of people, who had been transformed into fish and trees. As you've probably guessed, he gets help from Comfortable Camel, Speedy, and lots of other friends. THOMPSON and NEILL, 1930.

Pirates in Oz

Here comes Peter, another lone voyager from the United States, to adventure all over the Nonestic Ocean with Captain Salt and his pirate crew, and finally to sail to the Land of Oz and the Emerald City. Captain Salt and his pirates are not very much like the pirates you've read about in *Treasure Island*. They are so busy having magical adventures and exploring strange lands that they just can't spare the time to rob and plunder. Different, too, is their chef. He sails with them six months of the year because he likes to cook and travel, and stays home the other six months in his castle where he is none other than King Ato. And here's where you'll meet Roger the Read Bird. THOMPSON and NEILL, 1931.

The Purple Prince of Oz

This story is something like the old fairy tales in which the prince has to accept challenges, conquer, and perform feats of daring before he can become king or win the beautiful princess. Prince Randy of Regalia finds himself in just such a situation, and he courageously sets out to perform all the feats required of him. He wins the friendship of Kabumpo the elegant elephant, and after enough encounters to fill ten Oz books, he proves himself every inch a king. You'll like Randywell Handywell Brandenburg Bumpadoo, the Prince of the Purple Mountain. THOMPSON and NEILL, 1932.

Ojo in Oz

One day as Ojo sits quietly in the cottage in which he and his Unk Nunkie live, along comes a band of gypsies and lures him into one of their rattle-trap wagons. In no time at all, Ojo is their captive and the wagon carries him away from home. But why do the gypsies want Ojo? How is he, a small boy, in any way valuable to them? The surprise answer is worth waiting for. Ojo and his friend Snufferbux, a dancing bear and also a captive, are rescued from the gypsies by Realbad the forest bandit. Ojo and Realbad become very fond of each other and adventure through the Munchkin Country, visiting Unicorners, Crystal City, and other strange places. THOMPSON and NEILL, 1933.

Speedy in Oz

Remember Speedy, the little boy who arrived in Oz by space rocket from Long Island in *The Yellow Knight of Oz*? Well, here he is in his own book with a most delightful companion. Terrybubble is an honest-to-goodness live dinosaur, with all the lovable characteristics of a faithful dog. Speedy and Terry visit the fascinating islands—Umbrella and Roaraway—and are instrumental in freeing Umbrella Island of the tyranny of Loxo the terrible giant. Eventually they arrive in Emerald City. There Speedy meets many old friends and Ozma uses her magic to send him happily home again to his beloved Uncle Billy. THOMPSON and NEILL, 1934.

The Wishing Horse of Oz

Most Oz fans are mystery fans, too, so here is an Oz mystery that is all tangled up in three strands of emeralds and the strange magic that lies in the depths of their stones. Originally intended for a tree maiden, they instead fall into evil hands. The story starts in Skampavia, a tiny country outside Oz, where Skamperoo, the ambitious and discontented king, decides to become king of all Oz. He succeeds, for a time. His companion is Chalk, the magnificent white wishing horse, and it is the good horse sense of Chalk that brings about the happy final chapters of this book. Skamperoo is sent contentedly back to Skampavia. THOMPSON and NEILL, 1935.

Captain Salt in Oz

Samuel Salt, Captain of the "Crescent Moon," once a pirate ship and now the royal exploring ship of Oz, makes a number of exciting discoveries. First, he finds Tandy, boy king of Ozamaland, living in a jungle where he had been left to the mercies of the Leopard Men by Boglodore, a wicked magician. Captain Salt then actually discovers Ozamaland, a fabled country of flying reptiles, and of elephants, camels, and a fabulous White City. The evil Ozamandarins who steal Tandy's throne are brought to justice. Tandy leaves his good friend Chunum to rule his country while he completes his royal education as cabin boy of the "Crescent Moon." THOMPSON and NEILL, 1936.

Handy Mandy in Oz

How many times have you heard people say, "I've only got two hands"? Handy Mandy never says that, for she has seven hands—all of them useful. When this former goat-girl arrives in Oz, she becomes the close friend of Nox, a white Keretarian ox. Working together, Handy Mandy and Nox succeed in freeing the hapless little King Kerry from his captors, and in placing him on his rightful throne. All this takes a lot of doing, but Handy Mandy is in there pitching with all seven hands. When you read *Handy Mandy* you probably will become very fond of the little girl who came to Oz on a flying rock. THOMPSON and NEILL, 1937.

The Silver Princess in Oz

Even kings are victims of "adventuritis," and young King Randy of Regalia, whom we have met in other Oz books, is no exception. He just leaps from his throne to the back of his royal elephant, the elegant Kabumpo, and starts off to visit his old friend Jinnicky, Red Jinn of the Land of Ev. Long before they arrive at Jinnicky's castle, Randy and Kabumpo are breathless with all that can happen only in Oz. They pass through an amazing chasm called Gapers' Gulch, meet Planetty, lovely Princess from Anuther Planet and Thun the Thundercolt, her amazing steed. (They like the space maiden and her other-world horse so well that they take them along with them.) But this is just the beginning of a story that is truly "out of this world." THOMPSON and NEILL, 1938.

Ozoplaning with the Wizard of Oz

Of course you have heard of the stratosphere—who hasn't, nowadays, when talk of space travel seems just a breath of air away from the actuality. In this tale the Wizard of Oz invents ozoplanes, wonderful magical craft that zoom up into the stratosphere. As you may suspect, the stratosphere over Oz is different from any other. Here the stratosphere boasts a country called Stratovania, ruled by King Strut. This high-minded monarch takes a fancy to Jellia Jamb, new arrival by ozoplane, and decides to make her his Starina. Simultaneously, the occupants of another ozoplane are adventuring on Red Top Mountain, where Bustabo has stolen the throne from Azarine. THOMPSON and NEILL, 1939.

The Wonder City of Oz

Jenny Jump is a girl from New Jersey who becomes involved with an Irish fairy, a leprechaun, who unwisely gives Jenny just enough magic to make her unreasonable. Whenever Jenny becomes angry, which is often, she jumps. Finally, she becomes very angry and jumps clear to Oz. Actually, Jenny is very lucky for she finds a magic "turn-style." Those who pass through the turn-style come out in newly-styled clothing. Jenny gets the help of a small boy, Number Nine, to run a style shop, but none of this is enough for Jenny. She wants to rule all Oz. Of course something has to happen and it does. And her leprechaun is persuaded to confine his green magic to New Jersey where the natives regard it with no more wonder than they do their mosquitoes. NEILL, 1940.

The Scalawagons of Oz

After the success of his ozoplanes, the Wizard of Oz decides to invent something for both land *and* air travel. The result is scalawagons. Everything is running smoothly when Tik-Tok, superintendent of the Scalawagons Factory, runs down. Along comes the Bell-snickle, a mystery even to himself, and takes advantage of Tik-Tok's helpless condition by loading the scalawagons with flabber-gas. The Wizard hasn't counted on this and nearly loses all his scalawagons. It takes a whole book—filled with the fascinating adventures of Jenny Jump, the Nota Bells, a rubber ghost, and a Mifkit—to tell the story of the rescue of the scalawagons. NEILL, 1941.

Lucky Bucky in Oz

Lucky Bucky, a small boy from the United States, is aboard a tiny tug boat in New York Harbor not far from the Statue of Liberty, when the boiler of the tug boat blows up. Lucky is blown sky-high and into a whole "bookful" of of wonderful adventures. First of all, he meets Davy Jones, a wooden whale, who gladly accepts Lucky as a passenger. The inside of Davy is furnished as elaborately and comfortably as an ocean liner. Lucky and Davy go plunging all the way to the Emerald City, meeting many strange people on this water-level route to the Land of Oz. This is the first time we ever heard of a whale in a river, but maybe that's what makes it a whale of a tale. NEILL, 1942.

The Magical Mimics in Oz

For thirty years, from 1913 through 1942, there had been a new Oz book each year. But in 1943 John R. Neill, life-long illustrator and author of the last three Oz books, died. America was at war, and paper was difficult to obtain even in limited quantities. For four years no new Oz book was published. In 1947 *The Magical Mimics in Oz* appeared, the work of a new author and a new illustrator. Here is Oz once again, and in the best Baum tradition.

The sinister, colorful Mimics, winging from out of the depths of Mount Illuso to capture Dorothy and the Wizard, the excitement in the Emerald City while Dorothy and the Wizard are captives of the Mimics, the discovery of Princess Ozana and her beautiful Story Blossom Garden—all go to make this one of the popular Oz books. SNOW [JACK] and KRAMER [FRANK] 1947.

The Shaggy Man of Oz

Ever since he met Dorothy on the road to Oz many years ago, the Shaggy Man has been one of the best loved of Oz characters. This book is Shaggy's story: how his famous Love Magnet falls from the gates of the Emerald City, and how Ozma explains to Shaggy that the valuable talisman can be repaired by only one person—the magician who made it. On his way to see this magician, Conjo, who lives on an island in the Nonestic Ocean, Shaggy meets Twink and Tom, twins from Buffalo whom Conjo had transported to his island. Adventure follows adventure, first in Conjo's Castle, then in the Valley of Romance, later in the caverns of the Fairy Beaver King, and finally even under the Deadly Desert. (There is a rumour afloat that Conjo again has the idea that he should be the new Wizard of Oz.) SNOW and KRAMER, 1949.

The Hidden Valley of Oz

This is the story of Jam, a small boy from Ohio, who journeys to Oz by means of a "collapsible kite." Jam lands in a jam indeed when his kite lets him down in Hidden Valley. There he becomes the prisoner of Terp the Terrible. The cruel giant has enslaved all the inhabitants of this beautiful Gillikin valley. Aided by his friend Percy the white rat, Jam escapes, but only to return after many adventures, and reduce Terp to normal size, thus freeing the grateful people of Hidden Valley. Ozma sends Jam home to Ohio, while Percy, now human being size, prefers to stay that way in Oz. New characters whom Jam meets on his travels are the Rhyming Dictionary and the Leopard with the Changing Spots. COSGROVE [RACHEL R.] and "DIRK" [DIRK GRINGHUIS] 1951.

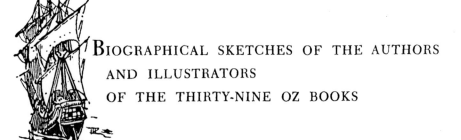

BIOGRAPHICAL SKETCHES OF THE AUTHORS AND ILLUSTRATORS OF THE THIRTY-NINE OZ BOOKS

L. Frank Baum (1856-1919)

On May 15, 1856, Lyman Frank Baum was born in Chittenango, a small town in Madison County, eight miles northeast of Syracuse, New York. Originally, the family bore the name of Van Baum and came from the Netherlands to America before the Revolutionary War.

When Frank was five years old his father, Benjamin Ward Baum, established the family home, called Roselawn, just outside Mattydale, a few miles north of Syracuse. Baum's father had made his fortune by developing Pennsylvania's first oil wells. (At one time, he had a young man on his payroll named John D. Rockefeller.)

Roselawn was the boyhood home that Baum knew and loved so well. He writes of it, calling it by name, in *Dot and Tot in Merryland*. Baum's writing ability manifested itself early. Between his twelfth and fifteenth years he wrote, edited, and published the *Roselawn Home Journal*, a newspaper which was widely circulated throughout Syracuse and which carried advertising by local merchants. It was printed on a "toy" press bought by Baum's father in New York; actually, this press was the equal of many used on country weekly newspapers.

Except for a rather unhappy season at Peekskill Military Academy, Baum was privately tutored, and through his love for books he was to a large extent self-educated.

His seventeenth year found Frank Baum an eager cub reporter on a New York newspaper, the old *World*. From this time on, his career varied to an almost bewildering degree. At the age of nineteen he opened a printing office in Bradford, Pennsylvania, establishing a paper which is ancestor to the present *Bradford*

Era. In 1880, at twenty-four, he opened and managed the Opera House in Olean, Pennsylvania. Perhaps the Baum zeal was too warm; in any case the Opera House went up in flames that very year. In 1881, Baum's first dramatic work, *The Maid of Arran*, was produced in Syracuse. It was so successful that it spent two prosperous years on the road. During the next two years, Baum wrote and played leading roles in such plays as *Matches* and *The Queen of Killarney*, using the theatrical name Louis F. Baum. Showbills of that period reveal him as a dark-haired, dark-eyed young man, well built and displaying the flowing mustache popular with his generation. According to newspaper reviews, Baum was perfectly at home on the stage—a good actor with a pleasant voice and courtly manner.

In the midst of these two busy years, Baum paused long enough to marry Maud Gage, a Fayetteville (New York) girl, who had just completed her sophomore year at Cornell. The wedding took place in Syracuse in 1882. In December, 1883, Frank Joselyn Baum was born, and the proud father decided the stage was no place for a family man. He settled in Syracuse in the retail oil business, selling "Baum's Axle Grease".

In 1888, with two sons now (Robert Stanton Baum had arrived in 1886), Frank could be held down no longer; the oil business was not romantic enough for him. He packed up his wife and children and went to Aberdeen, South Dakota, then a booming frontier town. Here he opened (and closed) Baum's Bazaar, a notion store. He started the *Aberdeen Saturday Pioneer*, soon closing it because, as he said, "The sheriff wanted the paper more than I did." Two more children, Harry Neal and Kenneth Gage Baum, were born in Aberdeen.

In 1890, with a wife and four boys to support (the oldest seven), Baum entered on a time of hardship and adversity. At thirty-four, with a comparatively crowded career behind him, Baum was reduced to selling crockery and chinaware "on the road". As a "drummer" or traveling man, he went by slow train and horse and buggy from one little middlewestern town to another. But he managed to support his family without help from his mother, who continually pleaded with him to return to Syracuse.

Eventually, things began to look up. Baum had found a writing job on the *Chicago Evening World*. There he remained until 1897, at which time he was able to make one of his dreams come true. Fortunately, this time it was a practical dream—a monthly magazine for window trimmers and merchants who relied on displays to sell their goods. Baum named it *The Show Window*. It filled a definite need and was immediately successful. Baum proved to be an energetic editor, overflowing with ideas and suggestions. The Baum family had achieved security, if not affluence.

The most important thing that had happened to Baum on the *World* was his meeting with W. W. Denslow, an artist working on the paper. Born in the same year and with a mutual interest in books, art, and the theater, they became firm friends. For the preceding ten years Baum had been contributing jingles, poems, and short stories to magazines, with only an occasional acceptance. As a writer, he appeared to be getting nowhere. His first book, *Mother Goose in Prose*, was published in 1897, but it failed to sell. In 1898, Baum wrote and Denslow illustrated *Father Goose: His Book*. Published in 1899, it was an immediate success, with no one more surprised at its amazing popularity than Baum and Denslow. They followed it swiftly with a book called *The Wonderful Wizard of Oz*. About the *Wizard*, Baum wrote to his brother, "I think it is the best work I have done, but you never can tell about the strange, queer public."

The public's opinion of *The Wonderful Wizard of Oz* is history; Baum and Denslow had arrived, but they were destined to do only one more book together —*Dot and Tot in Merryland*, published in 1901.

Baum naturally regarded Oz solely as his creation, but Denslow insisted that his work as illustrator was fully as important and that he should share in the profits of such enterprises as the tremendously successful stage play *The Wizard of Oz*, based on the book.

When *The Marvelous Land of Oz* was published as a sequel to *The Wizard* in 1904, it was illustrated by John R. Neill. In Neill, Baum and his publishers had found the virtually perfect artist to depict the fanciful wonderland of Oz and its whimsical people.

The remainder of the Baum story is one of almost unbroken success. Once he had public approval of his work, Baum wrote prodigiously. Lest readers suspect him of over-writing, he used seven different pen names. As Edith Van Dyne, he wrote the "Aunt Jane's Nieces" series of books for girls. As Floyd Akers, he wrote the "Boy Fortune Hunters" series for boys. As Laura Bancroft, he wrote *Policeman Bluejay*, one of his finest fairy tales, later reissued under his own name as *Babes in Birdland*. As Schuyler Stanton, he wrote two adult novels, *The Fate of a Crown* and *Daughters of Destiny*.

In 1906, Maud and Frank went abroad on a leisurely tour of Italy, North Africa, and Egypt. This was a vacation, but out of it came a novel—*The Last*

Egyptian, published anonymously by the Edward Stern Company of Philadelphia. Mrs. Baum once stated that Frank never ceased writing during the entire trip. When they were in Italy, Frank, who smoked a great many cigars—against doctor's orders—wrote home to a friend, "The only thing around here that smokes more than I do is Vesuvius."

In 1910, Baum moved his family to Hollywood, then a sleepy suburb of Los Angeles. He built a house, Ozcot, with a large garden and an aviary in which he wrote, while his birds perched on his shoulders and sang to him. When he wasn't writing, he was working in his garden. His flowers won so many prizes that he became known as the Dahlia King of California.

Wonderland pursued Baum. The motion picture industry grew up and surrounded the Baum home. Early pictures were made with Baum's garden and back fence used as setting for scenes.

In 1918, Baum suffered from a heart ailment. For a long year, he was either in great pain or just managing to rest comfortably. One night in 1919, Maud sat at his beside and the two talked quietly. Frank told her that he believed the end was near and that he had completed the manuscript for *Glinda of Oz,* his last Oz book. They talked of many things: their long and happy years of love and companionship, Maud's security, and of her plans for the future.

Before the night was out, at sixty-three, one of America's greatest writers of stories for children had passed on—on to Oz, or wherever it is that the great and good souls of this world go.

W. W. Denslow (1856-1915)

WILLIAM WALLACE DENSLOW was born in Philadelphia and received his early schooling in that city. The opening years of his career were divided between Philadelphia and New York, as he endeavored to establish himself in commercial art.

Something of a "gay blade," Denslow was a familiar and handsome figure as he frequented those restaurants and theatres in vogue as the playground for artists, writers, and actors of his day. He had a speaking acquaintance at least, with Sir Henry Irving, Bram Stoker, and the internationally known Ellen Terry.

In 1886, Denslow moved to Chicago, where he settled down to routine work as a newspaper artist. The Chicago of that period was blossoming as an art and literary center rivalling New York, and it was natural that Denslow should seek out and know the people who moved in these circles. When L. Frank Baum settled in Chicago, he and Denslow—as fellow workers on the *Chicago Evening World*—became friends. Out of this friendship popped a book of jingles by Baum, hilariously illustrated by "Den." The two men submitted this joint effort, *Father Goose: His Book*, to just about every likely publisher in the country. Finally, in 1899, it was only by putting up their own money that they persuaded a Chicago publisher, the George M. Hill Company, to publish and distribute the book.

The result created a sensation in the book world. Nearly 100,000 copies were sold in its first year.

In the year following, the Baum-Denslow collaboration team produced *The Wonderful Wizard of Oz*. The two men were now established in their careers as author and illustrator. In 1901, *Dot and Tot in Merryland* made its debut, perhaps the most delightfully illustrated of all the Denslow books.

But the storm clouds were gathering. In 1902, the musical extravaganza, *The Wizard of Oz*, opened at the old Majestic Theater on New York's Columbus Circle. At that time the Majestic was a brand new playhouse. The play, which bore almost no resemblance to the book, was a resounding success. Denslow believed that as illustrator of the book, he should share in the proceeds of the play. Neither the producer nor the author of the play agreed.

Thus, the Baum-Denslow collaboration was ended. Denslow went East and worked for a time with the Elbert Hubbard group at East Aurora, New York. He was a staff artist on the *New York Herald*. During these years, he wrote and illustrated a series of delightful nursery books: *The ABC Book, The Night Before Christmas, Humpty Dumpty, Little Red Riding Hood, Animal Farm*, and many others. He also wrote and illustrated *Billy Bounce*, much in the style and format of the Oz books. With Paul West, he wrote and illustrated *The Pearl and the Pumpkin*, which was translated into a Broadway musical comedy with only minor success.

Denslow even wrote and illustrated a small book called *The Scarecrow and the Tin Man*. Of course, the word "Oz" was not used in it. Ironically, a reprint of this little book was sold in the lobbies of New York theaters showing the motion picture *The Wizard of Oz*, a few years ago.

·Denslow's later years were not pleasant ones. Ill and unable to work at the end, he died penniless in Buffalo, New York, in 1915.

John R. Neill (1877-1943)

John R. Neill was born in Philadelphia on November 12, 1877, of Irish, Scottish, and Holland-Dutch ancestry. After completing high school, he attended the Pennsylvania Academy of Fine Arts, where he received his only formal art training.

Upon leaving the academy, he entered the field of newspaper illustrating, working for the *New York Evening Journal*, the *Philadelphia Inquirer*, and the *Philadelphia North American*. While on the staff of the latter paper, when he was but twenty-five, Neill illustrated his first Oz book, *The Marvelous Land of Oz*, a sequel to *The Wonderful Wizard of Oz*, which had been published four years before in 1900. The second Oz book was an immediate success; even today, as *The Land of Oz*, it is a "best seller" among Oz titles.

There were many who mourned the passing of the Baum-Denslow partnership, which had resulted in such delightful books as *Dot and Tot in Merryland; Father Goose: His Book;* and, of course, *The Wizard*. But it took only a few Oz books to establish Neill as admirably talented for depicting the famous Baum characters.

While Neill worked on his superb drawings and paintings for *The Road to Oz* and *The Emerald City of Oz*, he also illustrated *Evangeline, Snowbound*, and other classics.

At this time, Neill was undoubtedly strongly influenced by the great English illustrator, Arthur Rackham, as were many other artists of the period. The Neill style is one which combines rare beauty with great charm and a captivating sense of humor.

In all, Neill illustrated thirty-five Oz books, of which he also wrote three; he also illustrated other Baum books: *Sky Island, The Sea Fairies, John Dough and the Cherub*, as well as a series of six small books known as "The Little Wizard Stories of Oz."

Neill once remarked that he considered the Oz books merely a pleasant annual chore, and that he had no idea of the books' importance to their readers until he wrote *The Wonder City of Oz*. During all these years, Neill was also illustrating magazine stories for the *Saturday Evening Post*, the *Ladies Home Journal*, and other national magazines.

His home, in the early part of his career, was at Devil's Acre, bordering the upper Delaware. Later, he built a home on Long Island which included a studio for himself and a small theater. Here his four daughters staged plays for which he devised and painted the scenery. The latter years of his life were spent at his country home near Flanders, New Jersey, which bore the "Neillish" name of Endolane.

His daughters, now grown women, were models for many of the children who still adventure in the "Never-Never-Grow-Older" Land of Oz. It is typical of John R. Neill, who reflected the beauty of the world in pictures, that he often made a small design even of his name, with John contracted to the now quaint "Jno."

Ruth Plumly Thompson (1900-   )

LIKE John R. Neill and W. W. Denslow, RUTH PLUMLY THOMPSON was born in Philadelphia. At seventeen, she was selling verse and fairy tales to the fondly remembered *St. Nicholas* magazine. One year later, she was a staff member of *St. Nicholas,* and editor and writer of a weekly page for children for the *Philadelphia Ledger.*

When L. Frank Baum died in 1919, the publishers of the Oz books began looking for someone to continue the series. Miss Thompson's work in *St. Nicholas* attracted their attention. Her first book for the series, *The Royal Book of Oz,* appeared in 1921. From then until 1940, she wrote an Oz book a year—nineteen in all. Miss Thompson gave up adventuring in Oz to write other children's books and articles, and to devote her time to television and radio projects.

In addition to the Oz books, Ruth Plumly Thompson is widely known as the author of ten fairy tale volumes, scores of verses, serials for juvenile magazines, syndicate features, magazine fiction and articles, radio and television scripts, and teen-age fiction. She now makes her home in Ardmore on the Philadelphia Main Line.

Jack Snow (1907-   )

BORN August 15, 1907, in Piqua, Ohio, of Irish, German, and American-Indian ancestry, JACK SNOW was 12 years old when L. Frank Baum died. He immediately wrote to Reilly and Lee, suggesting that he be commissioned the new author to write the Oz books. A polite person on the staff of

Reilly and Lee answered his letter, telling him he might have to wait a few years.

While he was a sophomore in high school, Snow originated and wrote the nation's first column of radio review for the *Cincinnati Enquirer*. After graduation, he served for a year as reporter and feature writer for the *Piqua Daily Call*. Then followed a brief period at Indiana State Teacher's College in Terre Haute, Indiana, and a part-time job at radio station WBOW. Eventually, this led to a radio career at WCKY in Cincinnati, and WING in Dayton, Ohio (which station he named). A hitch in the army as sergeant in the Air Corps was succeeded by seven years in the studios of the National Broadcasting Company, New York.

In the field of fiction, Snow has sold short stories and articles to leading magazines; a book of his collected short stories, *Dark Music*, was published in 1946. His unflagging interest in the Land of Oz—an enthusiasm which began in early childhood—has resulted in a collection of Baumiana and Oziana which is probably the largest owned by any individual.

[The foregoing has been prepared by Himself (an Irish cat), and ALBERT J. QUINN—a fellow Baum enthusiast.]

Frank Kramer (1909-   )

BORN in New York, FRANK KRAMER gave up a business career to become a free lance artist simply because he has always liked to draw and paint. Once he found the courage to turn his back on the business world (and its salary check which turned up with reassuring regularity twice monthly), he found that there was a very real use for his talent in story illustration.

Kramer first made a name for himself in Street and Smith magazines. His sports illustrations were extremely well done, perhaps for the very good reason that Kramer has always been an ardent Dodger fan. His flair for the imaginative led to his illustrating two Oz books—*The Magical Mimics in Oz* and *The Shaggy Man of Oz*. Currently Kramer's work may be seen in many of the most widely circulated national magazines.

The unpretentious Kramers live a good Brooklyn life in a modest apartment and drive a low-priced car; to all appearances, Frank might still be the "typical" business man he started out to be, instead of an artist whose work is known nationally.

Rachel R. Cosgrove (1922-   )

Born December eleventh—uncomfortably close to Christmas, according to Miss Cosgrove—at Westernport, Maryland, Rachel Cosgrove attended schools in Maryland and West Virginia. She graduated from West Virginia Wesleyan College (Buckhannon) with majors in biology and public speaking and with the degree Bachelor of Science.

Occupation-wise, Miss Cosgrove does pharmacological research for a large pharmaceutical concern near New York City. Her job classification is that of chemist.

The Land of Oz was the first Oz book Miss Cosgrove read; at the early age of five years, it made such an impression on her that it still remains her favorite Oz book (with the possible exception, of course, of *The Hidden Valley of Oz*). Her likes run in the B's—Baum—bowling—bridge—and she has an understandable weakness for cats of high or low pedigree, and for white rats, like Percy.

"Dirk" [Dirk Gringhuis] (1918-   )

Dirk Gringhuis was born in Grand Rapids, Michigan, of Welsh-Dutch descent. When he was a little boy and grown-ups asked him, "What do you want to be when you become a man?" Dirk always answered that he wanted to be an artist.

He began his career by studying under several painters. In 1939, he studied illustration at the American Academy of Art in Chicago; after two years there, he went to New York City for further study.

In 1942, Dirk, now married, returned to Grand Rapids, where advertising art beckoned. In 1946, he did his first juvenile illustrations. This outlet for his talents so fascinated him that he decided to devote all his time to it. In 1947, he moved to the tulip town of Holland, Michigan, where he wrote and illustrated his first book. Since then, he has written three more books for children, worked as a free lance illustrator, and headed the art department at Hope College.

Dirk now has a country home just outside Lansing, where he lives with his family, Mrs. Gringhuis, eight-year-old Rickey, a dachshund named Otto, and a cat with the incredible name of Tommasacio. For relaxation, Dirk paints portraits, takes an active part in an arts and crafts society, and in the Cub Scouts.

ALL RIGHTS RESERVED

COPYRIGHT © 2010

BLUE LANTERN PUBLISHING INC.

3645 INTERLAKE AVENUE NORTH • SEATTLE, WASHINGTON 98103

WWW.LAUGHINGELEPHANT.COM

A map of the marvelous LAND OF OZ-showin

the celebrated and magical countrie

...ts great protective desert barriers, and many of

- LAND OF EV
- ROSE KINGDOM
- DEEP CANYON
- HOTHOUSE
- BRIDGE
- Isle of Pingaree
- Nonestic Ocean
- Isle of Phreex
- CASTLE
- Track of the Magic Carpet
- OOGA-BOO
- Nome King's tunnel
- WHEELERS
- DOMINIONS OF THE NOME KING
- RINKITINK
- River
- Winkie Country
- Woodman's
- Winkie R.
- ttenhots
- Mr. Yoop
- rs
- Truth Pond
- Yips
- DEADLY DESERT
- Sand boat crossed here
- PHANFASMS
- WHIMSIES
- RIPPLE LAND
- Kingdom of Dreams
- GROW-LEYWOGS
- VEGE-TABLE KING-DOM
- VOE
- BOBO-LAND
- PYRAMID MT.
- WASTE
- COUNTRY OF THE GARGOYLES
- ODLERS
- Foxville

Drawn by Professor H. M. Wogglebug, T.E.

...hich lie beyond the parched sands

LaVergne, TN USA
08 February 2011
215731LV00006B/44/P